the Runaway

Outlaws & Orphans of Cooper's Ridge

CYNDI RAYE

The Runaway

Outlaws & Orphans of Cooper's Ridge
Book 1
by
CYNDI RAYE

Copyright © 2022 www.CyndiRaye.com[1] All rights reserved. No part of this publication may be copied, reproduced in any format, by any means, electronic or otherwise, without prior consent from the copyright owner and publisher of this book. This is a work of fiction. All characters, names, places and events are the product of the author's imagination or used fictitiously.

---

1. http://www.CyndiRaye.com

Dedication

<u>This book is Dedicated to Mike Enloe</u>

The son of one of my dear friends.

Thank you for taking on a child and giving her a father, someone to count on and love unconditionally. One of the greatest gifts of all time is to be there for another.

About The Runaway
A Man With A Shameful Past - A Woman Forced From Her Home - Can Two Outcasts And An Orphan Build A New Life Together In Cooper's Ridge?

Marie Wilson feels like the bad side of Cinderella living with her step-mother and step-sister who make her life miserable. When she is forced to leave home, a new life waits for her in Texas.

Except it's not the life she imagines. Finding herself in a unique situation, she agrees to step in as a mail-order bride to help raise an orphan who would rather runaway than have someone love him. Can she put her own dreams aside to make a new life with strangers?

The new doctor, Owen Gorden, has a shameful past he's trying hard to come to terms with. When he orders a boy from the Orphan Train and a new mail-order bride for a marriage of convenience, the past seems to fade away. Or, has it? Will guilt cause him to spill the beans and ruin any chance with his new bride and family?

Outlaws & Orphans of Cooper's Ridge is a spin-off from Cyndi Raye's **Sons of Nora White** series.

Cooper Murphy wore many badges in his outlaw days after the war. When he realizes he was becoming like the outlaws he chased, he returns home to change his life. Now a rough-speaking, gun toting man of God, he buys a plot of land and slowly builds the town of Cooper's Ridge. But there are rules and regulations to follow. Cooper's Ridge is for those who were once sinful and now have redeemed themselves, wanting to build a new life in a town that won't shame a man for his past behaviors. Can he keep peace and help build a town filled with character and redemption?

Don't forget to visit www.cyndiraye.com for a free short story from Mail Order Brides of Wichita Falls series.

Chapter 1

Cooper's Ridge, Texas

Pastor Murphy nodded to his congregation. "Good Morning, folks. I'm going to step aside for a few minutes as one of our neighbors, Olivia Young, the founding member of the Orphan Train Committee , has an announcement to make." The preacher stood back and motioned for the young woman to rise. "Come front and center."

Owen Gordon sat three rows from the front, leaning back against the hard church pew as everyone in the congregation welcomed the presenter. Frankly, Owen wasn't happy with her organization one bit. He had a bitter pill in his mouth over the whole orphan train ordeal and wasn't in a mood to listen to her explanation, which he had demanded earlier when he spoke to the pastor in a private conversation.

Cooper Murphy was the owner of Cooper's Ridge as well as the town's pastor. He bought the land, had it platted and leased each building for two years to make sure the recipient followed the rules and regulations of the town's ordinances. After the renter proved he was indeed redeemed, Murphy sold the building for one dollar and the recipient became the new owner to do with the property as they wished. If the owner sold the building, it still had to fall under the town's guidelines. Cooper's Ridge general assembly kept strict rules on this.

Most of the men in Cooper's Ridge were former outlaws of one type or another after they saw the light of their ways. Some men, like Cooper himself, had been heading down a bad road and turned themselves completely around, except polite society wouldn't give them a second chance.

Owen was in that category. He had tried to redeem himself for two years after he accidentally shot and killed a man. Even though it was self defense, he had no witnesses to vouch for him. The only reason he didn't hang was because the town was desperate for a doctor. Even so, every single man and woman in his old hometown reminded him daily how they did him a great favor by not bringing in the hanging judge.

When a traveler visited his office one day he found out about Cooper's Ridge and decided to make the journey to a new life with people who understood what he had gone through. After six months living here, he knew without a doubt this was home. It was the place where he planned to start a family of his own and feel like he belonged somewhere.

Except the woman standing in the front of the church was rambling on about the mistakes made bringing orphans here. "As I said, there was an issue with a few of the children on the Mercy Train. Several of the children did not make it here and we are looking into that as I speak."

Owen, as the new doctor, felt it was his duty to speak for the others as well as himself. He stood out of respect and waited to be addressed.

"Greetings, Doc Owen. How can I help you?"

He nodded. "Greetings, Mrs. Young. I'm afraid that I'm the reason you are having to explain yourself today. I spoke with Pastor Murphy the other day because I had to close my practice early to meet the train in Mill Ridge expecting an orphan and to my surprise there was not one boy on the train. They were all girls and babies."

She nodded. "That's why I am trying to explain what happened. There was a mild disappearance at one of the orphanages we use. While most of the girls and babies came from The Children's Aid Society in New York City, we also were expecting a certain number of boys from the New York Juvenile Asylum."

"What does this have to do with my situation?" Owen didn't mind having to wait, especially since his mail order bride was only due next week, but he had agreed to adopt an orphan boy and wasted a whole day traveling for no reason when there were patients to see. That didn't sit well with him.

"Your situation is a rare one," she told him, smiling apologetically. "Several of the children ran away before the train left the station in New York City and had to be rounded up to travel at a later date."

One of the men in the congregation spoke up. "I don't know why the good doctor wants an orphan! Children who are thrown away are a source of corruption and very few are useful."

Owen turned towards the farmer. He wasn't fond of the man and was glad he only came to town on occasion. "Mr. Anderson, I'm of the mind that anyone can change given the chance. I took in an orphan because they also need a home and I plan to provide for a good one right here in Cooper's Ridge, along with a mail-order bride."

Mr. Anderson snorted. "You'll regret those quick decisions. You just mark my words, Doc. Mark my words."

Olivia Young's voice rose, causing everyone to settle down. Owen glanced her way and realized she was trying to keep order. "I do have some good news for you, Doc Owen. I was waiting to tell you after the service today. Since we are speaking of your situation right now, I'm happy to tell you that a telegram came this morning indicating the child you ordered was found and is being sent here as we speak, along with an agent of the Juvenile Society to make sure he arrives this time. They'll be coming in on next Wednesday's train."

"Thank you, ma'am. I appreciate the update and all you've done to fix things." Owen sat down, not wanting to make a spectacle of himself. After all, she did find the boy. It was an inconvenience since his bride-to-be was coming in on next week's train as well. He had wanted to deal with each one separately in order to get to know them. Now, it looked like they'd be here at the same time.

Owen guessed he was trying to make everything fall into place by having the boy come here first to get to know the town since living in New York City was far different than here. He wanted to give the orphan time to adjust. He should know nothing works out the way it's supposed to.

As far as the mail-order bride, they had conversed in writing several times and felt she was going to be an asset to his family. He'd think about her later. Right now all he wanted was everything to work out the way it was supposed to.

The pastor took his spot in the pulpit. "Thank you, Olivia. I am a believer that we all can make a difference and this mercy train idea has been a positive light for so many families who didn't have children and for those wanting more. In the Bible it clearly states to take care of widows and orphans and I'm proud of the fact that Cooper's Ridge is doing their due diligence. Thank you, Doc Owen, for taking in an orphan, along with a mail-order bride to help grow this town of which I am extremely proud of. Enough said. Let's move on to our morning scripture."

The pastor's voice faded out as Owen sat back in his seat once again, contemplating all he had taken on. When he came to

Cooper's Ridge six months ago, Murphy had taken him aside and assured him that he'd be able to buy the building that housed an office and living quarters when his two year period was up.

Owen had signed the lease and opened his practice. The first few weeks had been flooded with patients that hadn't seen a doctor in ages. Some folks in town had to travel into Mill Ridge or Wichita Falls for a doctor and didn't want to go that far, so they suffered without getting the help they needed. Now, everyone who didn't want to travel lined up in front of his office daily.

The practice wasn't making a lot of money but it was enough to pay the lease and have some extra for savings. He supposed when his mail-order bride got here, he'd have to dish out extra money for her clothes and needs as well as the child. Owen didn't mind though, but he knew he'd have to budget the money more. They'd have enough to get by, along with some savings he had from before. The important thing was having his own family.

What he found out pretty fast was not all patients paid with coins. Many of the women brought him so much food he had enough to last a month of Sundays. He was given milk, home-churned butter, fresh baked bread and cakes in lieu of payment and accepted it since most of the folks were also trying to build up their own business and lives.

When they brought him chickens he had to put a stop to those payments. He didn't have time to feed quacking birds and get chased around the yard while gathering eggs. Instead, he asked the owner of the chickens to keep them and bring him a few eggs instead. One middle-aged man looked at him as if he were crazy for refusing such fine birds, but Owen was adamant. He was a busy man.

Once a month he rode to Dallas in a rented buggy for more supplies at the apothecary shop. Luckily for him, he didn't have to send away for what he needed. The Dallas Apothecary had enough supplies to sell him and other smaller offices the important medicines they used in their practices.

While in Dallas, Owen usually spent the night in a hotel, along with a good supper at the hotel's restaurant. It broke up his life and gave him a chance to wear his Sunday best besides church. He assumed when he married his future bride, she'd come along with him. The orphan child, too.

Owen couldn't recall what the pastor preached about since he was too busy daydreaming. When everyone got up, he made his way outside, where the congregation was gathering in the side yard for some pastries and lemonade. Most of the townsfolk and neighbors mingled for an hour or so until they went on their way. The farmers in the area usually hung around longer since Cooper's Ridge was the only town close to their farms. They usually didn't get to mingle much with other people all week long while tending to their land and animals.

Owen was the opposite. He had a thriving business speaking to people on a daily basis. On Sunday, he stayed long enough to grab a pastry he liked before going on his way. It always seemed like the townsfolk wound up asking him medical questions the moment they saw him, so he tried hard to avoid them by leaving early. He needed a break away at times, too.

"Why, Doc Owen! How nice to see you here."

He stuffed a piece of the apple dumpling in his mouth so he wouldn't have to talk. He lifted a hand and waved, looking apologetically at the recipient. Most times, they did all the talking anyway and all he'd have to do is nod. Owen should feel bad but he honestly did not.

"I'm so happy to hear you are taking in one of the orphan children, Doc. My school is filling up rather quickly with our last batch of children and that pleases me immensely."

The teacher of Cooper's Ridge was fairly new. She came out here a few months before Owen had, along with her new husband who ran the gunsmith shop. Molly and Harrison Nelson were from a place called Noel, Kansas and were good friends with Cooper Murphy. They really weren't as bad or talkative as most of his patients.

Owen looked up to find the two of them watching him eat his apple dumpling. He tried to give a smile and another wave. "Excuse me, my mouth is full," he told them both.

"No worries, sir. We'll be on our way while you eat. Have a great day and make sure to come along on your new son's first day of school so I can register him and go over all the details with you."

That's if I ever get an orphan boy! He knew the committee was trying hard to make the Mercy Train work, but if an orphan was running away at every chance he got, Owen honestly wondered if the boy would be more trouble than what it was worth. He finished his apple dumpling and made his way down the street towards the livery. He was going to go on a long ride with his face in the wind, as he contemplated this new life he was about to start.

Cooper's Ridge had been a new start six months ago when he came here not knowing what to expect. Now, he was about to become a husband and father at the same time. Was he worthy of these new titles? He had killed a man and even though he thought he put it in his past, the nagging feeling that always arose when he wanted something more came to the surface.

Was Owen truly worthy enough to have his dreams come true of a family to call his own?

He saddled up the mare at the livery and headed out to open fields, gazing back to find Cooper's Ridge behind him.

With the wind in his face as the mare galloped through the field, he gave a nod to the man upstairs. Guess he'd find out next week if he was worthy or not.

Chapter 2

Manhattan, New York City

Marie Wilson stared out the window of the rich, chocolate-brown stately home her father owned. The Brownstone sat above the street with a regal staircase leading to the front porch. The banisters were trimmed with elegant carvings to match the entrance door. She gazed out into the streets to find several carriages passing by. It wasn't the busiest time of day, but Marie would rather be out in the sunshine instead of cooped up inside.

If her step-mother knew she was dallying, there'd be more work piled on her. Most likely work her step-sister Dora never finished. Which somehow happened every single day. There wasn't one day where Constance Wilson was forgiving of her step-daughter.

Marie pulled the heavy curtains together, spinning around when she heard footsteps coming closer, fear radiating through her whole body. Had she been caught?

"Marie! What are you doing? Day-dreaming again?" Her step-sister shook her head, which caused the woman's dark-haired ringlets to bob around like one of those toys in the window of the department store that had a spring and kept moving for a long time afterwards.

"I thought I heard a knock on the door." It was a blatant lie even though Marie knew she wouldn't be believed anyway. Marie's blonde hair was pulled back into a strict knot, pulling her skin tight, causing her eyes to slant slightly. Her step-mother insisted it was the proper way to wear her hair but Marie didn't think it was proper at all. The tight knot hurt her head more than anything.

She swiped a hand across her forehead. Her step-sister hated her and constantly tried to get Marie in trouble. It worked every single day. It didn't help that her father had decided his new wife would be the disciplinarian to both girls, allowing Constance to dish out punishment at her will.

Except Dora could do no wrong so it was always Marie who was accused of wrong-doing. As a result, she was given more work or denied a meal. She wasn't sure when the last time she had sat down at the supper table with her father. Sadly, he never noticed she wasn't present and if he did notice, he never said anything.

They hated her and wanted her gone. She knew her step-mother resented the fact that she looked so much like her mother, but Anna-Marie Wilson had been dead for four long years. She was no threat to Constance except the new wife didn't seem to think so. She wanted all traces of her father's former wife gone. That included Marie.

When Marie had complained to her father that Constance took down her mother's portrait in the hallway, he sat her down and explained how Constance felt threatened. Marie still didn't understand how anyone would be afraid of someone who was gone. Her mother had a right to be on that wall. She had earned it. Even though she put up a fuss, her father refused to budge on the matter.

Marie realized she was either going to have to find her own way in life now that she wasn't wanted here, or tolerate life with these two horrible women. Marie didn't know what to do. She had no money to go anywhere. Constance kept her working all day and evening so she couldn't find a job if she wanted to. The circle was never-ending and Marie didn't know how to get away.

Her father had suggested it was time for his daughter and step-daughter to think about a future of marriage. Which made Marie almost laugh. How was she ever going to win over a suitor with the ragged clothes she wore? She glanced at herself in the wall mirror as she stood next to Dora.

By comparison, Dora wore one of her frilly pink day dresses that accentuated her creamy white skin. Her hair was perfect with those tiny ringlets flowing down in perfect harmony. Marie stood beside her with a ragged shirt on, the sleeves rolled up from washing the floor and her skirt torn in a few places. She hadn't gotten around to sewing it yet. Even her kid boots were scuffed and worn.

"Mail call!" A few letters came sliding through the letter box connected to the front door, then footsteps faded away as the mail carrier went on to the next house. Dora turned to the huge wooden front door, bent down and picked up the pile of letters in today's mail. She shuffled through them, then came to a stop. "Here it is."

"What is it?" Marie was curious now. Dora was never nice to her. For her step-sister to even speak to her was alarming. What had she missed?

Dora realized she had spoken out loud and turned away when Marie tried to lean over her shoulder. "Mother! Mother! I caught Marie again!"

Marie wanted to stick a foot out and trip Dora, but knew she'd get into deeper trouble if she did. She picked up her skirts and ran towards the kitchen where the cook hid a basket of bread and cheese for Marie no one knew about. If she was going to be without supper, Marie would at least have something to eat.

Miss Ophelia was rolling dough onto the table when Marie hurried by. "Good day to you too, Miss Marie! It's on the bottom shelf this time," she called out.

Marie zig-zagged through the kitchen, bending down to grab the small basket of food and thanked the cook. "I love you, Miss

Ophelia!" She let the back door slam since no one would dare to go into the kitchen looking for her. Dora and her mother thought they were too good for that. She rounded the first floor brick wall and stepped into her beautiful vegetable and flower garden hidden between two outside walls. It wasn't a huge place, maybe seven hundred feet long and barely twenty feet wide, but it was Marie's domain.

She loved her garden. The sun shone through the clouds at just the right spot every single day and there was enough rain water to give the plants and flowers the nutrition it needed. She wasn't sure why it was her favorite place. Maybe because her mother loved it so.

She felt her mother's presence here. Marie walked to the prized rose bush and sat on the bench beside it staring at the beautiful deep red petals. Her mother spent many hours out here making sure this plant grew into the lovely plant it was today. Every year it bloomed enough roses where she'd proudly display them in a vase at their table.

Marie missed those days. She took a bite of the bread Ophelia packed in her basket. It was so fresh it melted in her mouth. If Marie was to leave, the only one she'd truly miss would be the cook. Everyone else had their own lives to live. Not even her father would care if she went away. Between her father's work at the bank and his new family, he had somehow forgotten about Marie.

The only problem was figuring out how to leave here. Where would she go? What would she do? Marie wasn't afraid of hard work, she scrubbed the floors and washed everyone's clothes and ran errands all day long until she'd fall into bed exhausted every single day.

If she was going to do that for the rest of her life, she wanted to be paid for it and live in her own house. Not with these horrible people who despised her anyway.

She began a one-sided conversation like she always did when she was in the garden. "I'm sorry, Mother. I wish I could stay here but it isn't meant to be. Some way, somehow, I have to leave. Maybe once I'm settled I can come back and dig up the rose bush and take it with me." No one would miss it anyway. At least it would be taken care of.

Marie sighed. She glanced at the upstairs window of her mother's old sewing room. It was the only window facing the garden. A dark shadow moved out of the way just as she glanced up. Marie stared hard. She stood, taking a few steps closer to the window. No one ever went into that room. It was locked. Her father had insisted it stay locked and no one, not even his new wife and daughter were allowed to enter.

At least her father still had some sense. But, there was definitely someone there. She took the food basket and hid it in one of the alcoves along the brick wall where she kept most of her shovels and shears for the garden and went back inside, determined to find the person invading her mother's private space.

Marie made her way up the back stairs to the third floor. She passed her father's bedroom and noticed the lock was no longer on her mother's sewing room door. Whoever was snooping around in there forgot to lock it back up. Maybe they were still inside. She took a deep breath before turning the marble handle and pushed open the door.

Marie didn't see anyone inside. She gazed around the room to find everything just the way her mother had left things. She swung around to make sure no one was in the hallway then slid inside.

This was the first time since her mother died that she'd been in this room.

The sheer magnitude of her mother's presence overwhelmed Marie. She felt her mother everywhere from an embroidered blanket flung casually over her rocking chair where she sat by the window looking at her garden to the many piles of sewing material sitting in baskets lined up on the table. She knew Father didn't want anyone in this room, but now that she was here, she couldn't possibly leave.

She missed her so much. Marie sat down on the rocking chair and leaned back, closing her eyes for a moment as she dreamed of a time not all that long ago when she'd sit by her mother's feet and watch her sew for hours and hours.

Her mother would sometimes tell her a story and other times she'd sing to Marie. The memory was so real Marie could almost hear her mother laughing softly in the background. She smiled, remembering the woman's sweet voice and missing her so much.

The laughter got louder. Marie popped her eyes open. That wasn't her mother's voice. She sat up and stared out the window where she could see the garden in all its glory. It was the reason her mother chose this room as her sewing room. What Marie witnessed appalled her. She jumped up from the chair and began to bang on the window.

"Stop! No! Please, no!" The two women in the garden looked up at the window. When they saw Marie standing there pounding on the window pane, they laughed even harder. Then they went back to pulling every single plant and flower from the rich soil, tearing the flowers from their stems. The rose bush was at the end of the row. She had to stop them. She fled from the room, leaving the door wide open as she ran down the stairs as fast as her legs would take her.

When she ran past Ophelia without a word, the older woman stopped what she was doing and followed Marie out the door.

Marie ran towards the rose bush, not caring when she pushed Dora out of the way. Dora screamed and began to cry while Constance began shouting at Marie to stop right now!

"Let my rose bush alone! Please, do not destroy that, too!" She was practically begging the two women right before she flung herself onto the bush and felt the thorns prick her skin. All she wanted was to protect the roses. She turned around and faced the two women. Dora was pretending to cry. "I didn't hurt you!"

"You pushed me! Mother, do something!"

Constance stared hard at Marie and shook her head. She lifted a finger and began pointing it at Marie. "I'm not sure why you have this secret garden hidden from us, but it will no longer be yours to do as you wish. This is appalling! Hiding things behind our back! How dare you?"

Marie had no answer for the horrible woman. She gazed at the mess the two women made. Plants and flowers were spread all over the ground, slowly withering away. At least her mother's rosebush was left intact. She got here just in time.

Constance was still pointing a finger at Marie. "There will be dire consequences for your horrible behavior, Marie. When your father hears what you've done, it wont surprise me if he sends you away!"

Marie was on the verge of tears. She lifted her chin in defiance. If she were to be sent away it might be better for all of them. Yet, she doubted Constance would want her gone since Marie was the one who did all the work. Marie couldn't imagine Constance lifting a finger to wash a floor or even clean the dust from the wooden tables.

"Do you have anything to say for yourself?"

What was she supposed to say? Sorry? Marie pursed her lips and stayed silent. She cast her eyes down to the ground, staring at the tips of Constance's shoes. She wasn't going to say a word. Not one word.

"Very well, then. Your father will decide what to do with you. After Dora is gone, it will be just you and I here until I find a way to get rid of you, too."

"Mother, it sounds as if you are happy I'll be leaving!"

"I'm happy you will be settling down with a good husband."

Marie was shocked. Dora was getting married? When did this happen? Was that why she was all excited about the letter that came today?

Dread filled Marie. If Dora was gone, Constance would not have anyone to keep her occupied. Except for Marie. Dear Lord, she had to find a way out of this horrible place. It was no longer home. Her father was too smitten to know what kind of woman he married.

Marie was alone.

She had to rise up and find a way to escape from here. One way or another.

Chapter 3

Two weeks later

Marie had been confined to her bed chambers for the last few weeks after her chores. Her step-mother gave her all of Dora's work plus her own, carefully keeping a close eye on every move Marie made. If she even tried to go near the garden, Constance or Dora would block her way.

They both laughed when Marie found out the rose bush was destroyed as well. "It's for your own good," her step-mother said. "You'll learn one way or another not to defy me."

By the end of the evening Marie was too exhausted to do anything more than fall into bed. Or, what was left of her bed. She no longer had a bedroom since Constance claimed she needed the space for her own sewing room. The woman didn't even sew. So, she made Marie move her own bed and a dresser to a broom closet behind the pantry in the kitchen. There was enough space for Marie's bed and a small chest of drawers. Marie managed to salvage her mirror from her room and set it on the dresser.

Marie was lying on her bed when there was a knock on her door. "You're wanted at the supper table." Ophelia poked her head inside. "Your father would like a word with you."

Marie was more confused than ever. Why would her father want to see her? After all this time, she doubted he cared what happened to her. Unless Constance was up to no good. Which was more likely than not.

Slowly making her way to the dining room table, Marie stared at her step-mother and step-sister before sitting to the right of her father. He glanced up as she came in the doorway, but then kept his eyes focused on his plate.

THE RUNAWAY

There was no plate for her. She didn't think she was invited to eat with them anyway. Her stomach growled while Constance grinned at her discomfort. Marie was upset that happened. She hadn't wanted her step-mother to know she was hungry.

It wasn't because she wasn't eating. Ophelia made sure there was always food laid aside for Marie. Her stomach was growling from not eating all day. She had wanted to get all the extra work done that Constance put on her today, so she forgot to eat. Marie wasn't sure what Constance would do to Ophelia if she found out the older woman was feeding Marie, but obviously the cook wasn't afraid of her stepmother. Either way, Marie wasn't about to correct her and tell her that she wasn't going hungry. Let Constance think what she wanted to.

"Father? Did you want to see me?"

He nodded and finished swallowing his food before placing his fork on his plate. He looked up at his daughter first, then to his wife and step-daughter. "As you know, Dora is leaving as a mail-order bride next week."

The news was quite shocking. A mail order bride? She had no idea. "I didn't know, Father."

He frowned, the indent on his forehead quite obvious. He placed his hands together and continued to stare. "I mentioned before that it was time for my daughters to become brides. Dora listened and has taken the initiative into her own hands and accomplished a miracle in such a short amount of time. You see, the banking business is quite volatile right now. I'm in jeopardy of losing quite a lot of business and money. I have to protect what I have."

She didn't understand what all this had to do with her. "I'm not sure I understand, Father."

"I told you she wasn't able to comprehend things."

Her father gave his wife a stern look and she quickly lowered her eyes to the table. Then, he continued to speak to Marie. She had a tiny bit of comfort in that. "Marie, since you haven't been able to find a husband, you will be escorting Dora on her journey to Cooper's Ridge, Texas."

"Escorting Dora? You want me to leave here, Father?"

He picked up his fork before nodding. "Yes, that's what I said. The gentleman Dora will be marrying sent a ticket for her and an escort. Your step-mother and I have decided that you will escort Dora to Texas and make sure she is safe as she gets to her destination."

The thought of traveling so far away was exciting and yet terrifying, especially having to go with her awful step-sister. "All I have to do is escort her there and then come back here?"

Her father put down his fork again. He stared at Marie. "You're step-mother thinks it will be in your best interest if you stay in Cooper's Ridge and make sure Dora is settling okay. From her inquiries there are jobs available where you can earn money for a ticket back. I'm afraid we can't afford to pay for your way back at this time."

"What? Why not? Father? I'm your daughter? Are you going to send me away and then leave me there to fend for myself?"

"You'll have your sister. Perhaps her husband will be kind enough to let you stay."

"She's not my sister!"

"This is why I told you it will be difficult, Lloyd. She's obnoxious and dares to defy any requests given."

"Now, now, Constance. It is just a complete shock. This is the first time we've had any type of financial difficulty. She'll come around."

They were discussing her as if she wasn't sitting right there at the table with them. Her life here was over. Even though she wanted to get away, what would happen when she got to Texas without any money. "Father, I have no money. What if Dora's husband won't take me in? Where will I stay?"

He nodded. "I'll make sure you have some money in case things do not work out even though I expect everything to work out as arranged, Marie. That means you have to try to get along with your sister."

"Yes, sir." At least he was going to give her some money in case she needed it. The thought of having to live with Dora and a new husband horrified Marie. She'd escort her to Texas and figure out something on the way.

As she laid in bed staring at the small oil lamp on her little dresser, Marie wondered what was in store for her. Would Texas be anything like New York? She had read it was a huge place with cowboys and cows and steers and horses everywhere. Even though she was hurt that her father was so ready to get rid of her, the thought of a whole new world and adventure was quite enticing.

She blew out the oil lamp and crawled back under the covers. The money her father would give her would at least give her other options. Marie smiled into the darkness. She had wanted to be free of her step-mother and sister for so long. It was sad she had to go across the country to start over but there was nothing left here for her.

No family.
No love.

No one. Except for Ophelia. The woman had taken such good care of her. She'd miss her most of all.

*****

Marie was up and ready to leave long before the train was due. She wanted to say goodbye to Ophelia before she left unsure she'd ever see the woman again. She grabbed the small carpet bag she owned filled with two sets of skirts and blouses and one extra pair of boots. Winters in the city got quite cold but she was told in Texas there was no need for heavy winter wear.

She slipped from her room, closing the door behind her and hoping never to see that room again. "Miss Ophelia?"

"Come here, girl. I have breakfast for you." Marie slid onto the stool and began eating heartily before her step-mother could interfere. Even though she was leaving hadn't stopped Constance from being cruel. For two days straight she had Marie pressing Dora's outfits so she could fit them in the trunk that was being sent along on the train.

For Marie, there was no trunk. All she owned was in her carpetbag. Sadly, the last four years had seen her beautiful gowns her mother made be given to Dora. At first, Marie hadn't minded until she was reduced to two skirts and a pair of blouses that were now so stained she was ashamed to wear them in public. Except she had no choice.

Ophelia reached under the counter and brought up a square package wrapped in brown paper with a tan ribbon tied around it. "Put this in your bag, hurry!"

"What is it, Ophelia?"

The older woman smiled. "A little something from me to you. Don't wear it until you're rid of Dora. Otherwise, she'll try to steal it from you."

"Did you get me a dress?" At Ophelia's nod, Marie set it carefully inside her carpetbag and closed it quickly. There was no way she was going to let Dora get her hands on this. It was special. "Thank you, Ophelia. I'm going to miss you most of all."

"This is the best thing to get you away from that witch!" They both giggled at her words. "I put a little something in the pocket of the dress. It should hold you over if anything happens."

"Oh my goodness, Ophelia. You didn't have to do so much for me?" She gave the older woman a hug and held onto her for quite some time.

Ophelia took her hands and gave them a squeeze. "I almost forgot." Once again Ophelia reached underneath the counter and handed Marie a small sack with a twig sticking out the top.

"What is this?" There was a tiny green bud on the end of the twig.

"It's your mama's rosebush. I went out and tried to salvage what I could. This little sprig was sticking out for all the world to see like it was declaring life over death."

Marie took the sack and tucked it into her carpetbag, letting one end open slightly so air could circulate around the live plant. She gave Ophelia another hug. "I'll never forget you."

"Go on, now. Get on that train and never look back, Marie. Remember, dear, always have a plan."

Marie was surprised when her father stood at the door waiting for everyone to load up on the buggy. "I'll be driving you to the station," he told them. As they went out the door, her father stopped Marie. He handed her an envelope. "As promised, here is some compensation to help you in a bind. It isn't much, so use it sparingly. I'm sorry it is all I have to give you."

"Thank you, Father." She waited to see if he would hug her or tell her he'd miss her, but he turned and went out the door. She held the envelope in her hand watching him go until someone began to tug at her hand.

Her step-mother pulled the envelope from her hand. "You don't deserve one bit of this! This will go to Dora!"

"I'm telling Father."

"Then I'll tell him how Ophelia gave you a package and some money. I heard it all. I was standing behind the door. Let the old bat give you what she's got. You will never get another penny from this household."

She turned on her heels to follow her husband.

"You are a horrible person," Marie finally mustered up.

Constance turned back and hissed, "I suggest you shut your mouth right now or Ophelia will be out on her ears without a job. Then how will she take care of that daughter of hers?"

Marie silently followed her step-mother out the door, clutching her carpetbag in one hand. She couldn't afford for Ophelia to lose her job and not be able to take care of her crippled daughter. She got on the buggy and was so tempted to let her father know she no longer had the money he gave her but she stayed quiet for Ophelia's sake.

As they were pulling away from the Brownstone, a door slammed. Marie looked up to see Ophelia coming out the door. She pulled off her apron, bunched it up into a ball and threw it at Constance's feet. Words were exchanged although Marie wasn't able to hear what was being said.

She gazed at her father who was looking straight ahead. Dora wasn't paying attention to what was going on in front of their house either. Marie watched in amusement and amazement as Constance pointed a finger in Ophelia's face and Ophelia leaned her head back and laughed. Then Ophelia turned and walked down the street, away from Constance.

Marie had the biggest smile on her face as she remembered what Ophelia had said to her earlier. Always have a plan.

Chapter 4

Long, tedious days of rocking and bumping and being thrown from one side of the seat to the other was taking its toll on Marie. At least now she had the bench to herself. After a day and a half of bumping against her step-sister and listening to her awful remarks, it was so nice that she was sitting somewhere else.

Dora was sitting comfortably in a parlor car attached to the rear of the train while Marie sat on a hard bench breathing in soot and smoke. On the first night they made their way to the dining car, an older couple motioned for them to sit at their table. The couple were heading home to Kansas with their oldest son, who was going to be running their company.

Dora had been intrigued from the start. She openly flirted with the son and charmed the older couple. Marie stayed silent, only answering questions when they were directed to her. No one seemed to even mind that she barely spoke at all.

The next day they were both invited to sit in their private car for the rest of the trip. Marie had heard that private cars were elegant and so much nicer and was about to make her way towards the rear of the train, when Dora stuck out her foot, causing Marie to stumble and fall onto the hard floor. She looked down at Marie and sneered. "Do not go to the private car. If you know what's good for you, stay right here in that seat!"

Dora turned, leaving Marie sitting on the cold floor of the train car as pain shot through her ankle. A small boy called out to her, pointing towards a fleeing Dora.. "It was her fault. I saw the whole thing."

"I felt the whole thing. Can you help me up?"

"I can't. They won't let me get up from this bench."

"What? Why not?" She was staring into the big brown round eyes of a young boy. He was as cute as a button and couldn't be more than six or seven years old. Choppy brown bangs hung down, almost covering his eyes.

He shrugged. "They think I'll run away."

She was curious and forgot about her ankle for a moment. "Will you?"

"Will I what? Runaway? Probably."

"Why would you do such a thing."

"Nobody wants me."

Such harsh words for a child. Marie was quite surprised to hear him speak that way. Yet, she understood. "No one wants me, either."

He kept staring at her. "Are you an orphan?"

She smiled, grabbing a hold of his bench and pulling herself from the floor since no one else seemed to come to her rescue. The conductor was busy standing outside checking tickets as others got on. "I'm not an orphan. I did lose my mother a few years ago, so I'm sort of one."

"Do you have a father?"

She nodded. "Yes, but he thinks it's time I make my own way."

The boy didn't say anything.

She motioned for him to scoot over after she noticed someone had already taken her seat. She quickly grabbed her carpetbag and shoved it under the bench the boy was sitting on. "Scoot over. I just lost my seat."

He tried but found it impossible. That's when Marie realized the boy was truly strapped to the bench.

She moved past him and sat on the far side. "Who did this to you?"

He shrugged. "I don't know. One of the agents. They got tired of chasing me when I ran away a few times."

"You kept running away?"

"Why not? No one is going to want an orphan like me."

Marie's heart broke at the child's words. Maybe her life hadn't been all that bad as she thought about the boy sitting beside her. "What's your name?"

"I don't have a name."

"You don't have a name? What do they call you?"

"Boy."

"That's a terrible thing to call you!" She stared at the boy for some time. "David. Your name is David."

"David?"

"Yes. Do you know why I've named you David?"

He shook his head.

"Let me explain. David is the name of the second greatest King in all of Israel from a long, long time ago."

"I don't even know where Israel is."

"You don't have to know. Do you know what else I can tell you about David the King?"

"What else?" He scooted closer until his rope kept him from moving too much.

Marie wanted to untie him but if he was a runaway, she didn't want to get thrown off the train for doing so. "David fought a giant named Goliath. He was ten times David's size. There were two armies and everyone laughed because David went up against the giant. He was tiny compared to Goliath, but David had the heart of a warrior. Do you know how he won against all the odds he was dealing with?"

The boy shook his head. She could tell he was intrigued.

Marie smiled. She leaned in and whispered to him as if he were the only one important enough to have this information. "He had a slingshot and took a stone and hit the giant so hard with the stone it knocked him over. Then he cut off the giant's head with his sword."

"Wow! I wish I knew David."

"Well, I'll tell you this young man. The reason I'm naming you David is because you remind me of King David. Do you know the name means beloved. God really loved David so much."

"I don't think God loves me at all." The boy's lower lip was quivering. She had wanted to make him feel better and now he was about to cry.

"Oh, no, David. God does love you."

"Then why won't anyone choose me? I was on the orphan train two times but no one wants me."

"Is that why you ran away?"

He nodded.

"I'm sorry, David. Without a name, it's almost impossible to find a good fit for you. Now that you have a name I believe it will be much easier."

He smiled. She hoped and prayed she was right. If he was from the orphan train, where was his escort? "Who is with you, David?"

The boy shook his head. "Mr. MacFarley brought me on the train but I kept running away so he tied me to a bench and paid the man with the hat on to watch that I don't escape."

Marie was shocked. "You mean he abandoned you?"

"I guess so. Whatever that means."

"It means Mr. MacFarley is not a gentleman. Just one moment, please." She got up and made her way to the conductor, who was at the front of the car counting heads. "Sir, a moment please?"

She spoke with the conductor and made her way back to the boy.

"Did he tell you I am bad?"

"No, he did not and I won't allow anyone to speak ill of you."

"Is that bad talk?"

"Yes, David, it is. There will be no more running away, do you understand? I found out that we are destined to both arrive at a depot in the town called Mill Ridge. It's where you're new family will be waiting when you arrive."

The boy didn't flinch. "You don't really think they will be waiting, do you? It's never happened before."

Marie wondered if he ever gave it a chance. "Now, David. Do not speak so ill of your new family. They will be waiting for you. The conductor assured me of that."

"I guess."

"Nonsense. They will be there and I'm happy to announce I will escort you to your new home. If that horrible man who abandoned you won't do it, then I've taken it upon myself to make sure you arrive safely."

"Why?" He tilted his head, watching her closely.

She smiled and patted his arm. "Why not? We are both basically orphans, David, and need to look out for each other. It's what people do."

He seemed satisfied with that answer so she leaned back and closed her eyes for a few moments. It was so hard to rest on a train, but in another few days they'd both be in Mill Ridge and she vowed to stay with the boy until his new family came along.

If her step-sister didn't like it, then she'd have to go on without her since she basically abandoned Marie anyway. A slight fear rolled through her from her shoulders to her knees. At least she had extra money from Ophelia even though Constance took the money her father had given her. She was so glad to be away from that horrible woman!

But Dora was just as bad as her mother, maybe even worse. She was spoiled and petty and wanted everything that Marie had. Over the two years since her father had remarried, Marie lost most of her jewelry and all of her pretty clothes. She had been resigned to menial labor and a life of cleaning up after those two women.

Now, she was free. There was no way she planned to stay with Dora and her new husband. From the moment she left the city Marie decided she wasn't going to live her life under Dora's thumb any longer. Even though she didn't know how she'd do it, Marie knew by the time she got to Mill Ridge, she'd come up with a plan.

She glanced at the boy to find him sleeping. His head and shoulders were leaning precariously against her, making Marie smile. She imagined the boy trusted no one. Not after being rejected so often. A small tug at her heartstrings had Marie placing her arm around his shoulders and pulling him a little closer. He snuggled against her and slept.

Marie had fallen asleep as well, only to wake up as the train was pulling into another station. "Folks, we're in Topeka, Kansas," the conductor announced. "Get out and stretch your legs and stop by the hotel on the corner for some home-cooking. The train leaves in two hours so don't be late getting back on board."

This was the first stop where they were able to finally get off the train to stretch their legs. She motioned for the conductor.

"Yes, ma'am?" he inquired, tipping his hat.

"What will you do with David? Will he be able to get off the train for a while also?"

The conductor frowned. "Who is David?"

"This young man. I've given him a Christian name."

"Very well. MacFarley called him Boy and that's all I knew him by. To answer your question, he will have to stay put and I'll get him a sack of food for supper."

Marie shook her head. "That will not suffice, sir. I'd like to become his escort for the rest of the trip. Please untie him so he can sit at a table and enjoy a meal."

"I'm not sure that's a good idea, ma'am. I been paid to make sure he gets to Mill Ridge, Texas."

Marie crossed her arms and stared at the man. "I'm not worried that you got paid, sir. I won't ask for any monies to escort him. You keep the money that horrible MacFarley gave you and let me take him off your hands. I plan to get off at Mill Ridge and will make sure he is taken care of during this trip."

The conductor shrugged. "If you insist, then I can't stop you." He looked happy to be rid of the responsibility.

"Please untie him."

The conductor removed the restraint from the boy and shook his finger. "Make sure you listen to this young lady, boy. She's now responsible to make sure you get to your destination. If you try to run away again and I catch you, then you'll ride in the cattle car the rest of the way."

His eyes got huge. "What's a cattle car?"

"It's a car filled with cows, steers and bulls, and bulls don't like anyone. They can get meaner than a rattlesnake. Just remember that, boy."

Marie spoke up. "His name is David."

The conductor tipped his hat again. "Pardon me, David. You best get moving if you want to eat at the hotel. Best food in town."

Marie's legs were a bit wobbly as she left the train and went towards the big hotel on the corner of the street. David allowed her to take his hand, which made her glad she had a good grip on him since she didn't want to have to chase him down if he tried to run away.

For the moment, Marie wasn't too concerned he'd flee. His belly was rumbling the last few miles and when he woke up he told her how hungry he was. He seemed excited when she told him they were going to sit down to a hearty meal.

"Promise me you won't try to run away, okay, David?"

He nodded. "I promise."

Even so, she was going to keep a good eye on him.

Chapter 5

"Dear Lord, what are you saying, Dora?" Marie was shocked out of her kid boots!

"You heard me! The private car is now being moved from the train and I'll be going to the Lazy R Ranch instead of Texas. I'll also be marrying Brian Jones instead of the settler in Texas. You'll have to tell Mr. Gordon when you arrive that I am not going to marry him after all!"

"You are a horrible person, Dora! You promised to be a mail-order bride! Maybe *you* should go there and tell him that you aren't going to marry him! Why should I?"

Dora rolled her eyes. "Because you are not coming with me to the ranch! I've got myself a rich rancher and that doctor in Mill Ridge can't compete. I mean, did he send a private car? No, he didn't. He is a doctor in some forsaken town that probably won't have much money to begin with. I can't settle for that when I've got a future as a rancher's wife!"

Marie stared hard at Dora. She was going to leave Marie high and dry in the middle of Kansas and the woman didn't care. "What about me, Dora? I'll be left there with no money and no place to go."

Dora shrugged. "You can marry him, Marie. A country doctor would probably suit you anyway, that's if he can get past your plain looks."

At this point Marie didn't try to get Dora back with angry words. After all, over the last two years she had to have skin as thick as the leather on her kid boots. Then, she remembered Ophelia's words about coming up with a plan. "Okay, Dora. I'll go to Cooper's Ridge and inform the doctor you won't be coming after all, but in order to do so I want the money that my father gave me and your mother stole as we were leaving."

Dora pursed her lips. "You are bribing me. How dare you?"

Marie smiled. "I dare you. Does the ranch family know you are headed to Texas to become a mail order bride?"

Dora's eyes got huge and she froze in mid sentence. Marie never stood up to her before. Not like this. "You wouldn't?"

"All I have to do is tell them and they'll see the terrible person you are!"

Dora fumed. She growled at Marie and pulled the now tattered envelope from her reticule, along with a few letters from the man she was supposed to be marrying. Shoving it at Marie, she turned to walk away. "I hate you," she whispered.

Marie sighed. What a mess.

"Why does she hate you?" David was still holding onto her hand and stared up at her, curiosity all over his young face.

"I suppose its not just me she hates, but everyone. She doesn't even like herself."

The whistle blew loud and clear as they made their way from the boarded walk to the depot. They found the seats they had before and Marie made David promise not to run away. She was glad to see the ropes that tied him down were no longer there.

David noticed as well. "I won't have to be all tied up any more?"

She nodded. "That's right, David, and remember you promised me you will not run away. I have to make sure you get to your new home."

The boy settled on the seat, kicking his legs back and forth. He was acting like a normal child now that he wasn't tied up like a wild animal. Marie had made the right decision. Once she delivered the child to his destination, she'd figure out what to do.

She dug into the envelope her father had originally given her, pleased to see a hefty amount of cash. It boiled her blood to know that Constance had taken this from her and given it to Dora. At least now she had it back.

Between the money her father sent along and the extra cash she got from Ophelia, she'd at least be able to stay at a boarding house until she found a job. She gazed down at the boy. Maybe she could find a position taking care of children.

What was Cooper's Ridge like, she wondered. Was it a small town where everyone was friendly like she read about in the newspaper? Or, was it a big city where people went about their way minding their own business. She was getting more curious the closer they got.

Marie checked David, and his eyes were closed. She smiled. He had eaten every bit of food on his plate and then asked for chocolate cake for dessert. The restaurant had displayed several cakes on the sideboard and he hadn't been able to keep his eyes off of the chocolate concoction until she asked the waiter for a slice. He gobbled it down followed by a small glass of milk. He probably never ate anything that tasty before and now he had a full belly and was fast asleep.

Now that she didn't have to keep a close watch on her charge, Marie opened one of the letters from the man waiting for her step-sister in Cooper's Ridge.

Dear Miss Dora Wilson,

Thank you for writing in response to my advertisement for a mail-order bride. Now that you've told me quite a bit about yourself, I'd like to take the time to tell you who I am. My name is Owen Gordon and I'm a medical doctor who has recently taken up residence in Cooper's Ridge, Texas. Before I came to Cooper's Ridge, I was a medical doctor in a small town in Oklahoma.

Cooper's Ridge is a very small town. I've been here for six months and the people make me feel like I am finally home. There are many men who want a second chance or to make peace with some of the wrongs they've done in life. It's a special place where men can start over and find a peaceful oasis.

As my wife, I would like to know if you would be able to attend to my patients as my nurse on occasion? It would be helpful but if you find you cannot assist me in my work, then I am perfectly fine with that and will hire an assistant.

If you find this type of life suitable, please write back and I'll send a train ticket for you and an escort with my next letter.

Sincerely,

Owen Gordon

Marie smiled. Mr. Gordon sounded like a nice man and being a doctor was an important profession. Sadly, Dora was jilting him and she had to be the one to tell him. She opened the next letter he wrote.

Dear Miss Dora Wilson,

I was pleasantly surprised to get your telegram instead of a letter. By the sound of your situation I am assuming you are wanting to travel here as quickly as possible. I have enclosed a ticket for you and one for your escort. I've also enclosed money for you to buy provisions along the way. I'll be looking forward to meeting you when you arrive in Mill Ridge on Wednesday the twenty-first.

Look for a tall gentleman with dark hair and some say a handsome demeanor. Most importantly, I will have the tip of a red handkerchief sticking out of my front shirt pocket so you know it's who I say I am. One can never be too careful.

Sincerely,
Owen Gordon

Marie was even more impressed. Mr. Gordon gave her a way to find him that only she would know. He was already taking care of his new bride. Except, she frowned when realizing that she wasn't the one he had been trying to keep safe. It was Dora!

Maybe she should pretend to be Dora and marry the gentleman! It sure would solve her problems at the moment. Except, Marie was not the type of person to be deceitful. Besides, the good Lord would chastise her before the man ever found out she was lying.

No, she was left with the job of telling Mr. Gordon that Dora wasn't coming. It literally made her ill to think how Dora had just run off with a practical stranger in the middle of a train ride. Her step-sister was heartless and cold. Marie was glad to be rid of her, but at the same time, sick that she had to be the one to tell poor Mr. Gordon. He seemed like a kind man. She just hoped he wouldn't be too disappointed.

*****

The conductor let out a shout over top of the screaming whistle. "Mill Ridge coming up next!" They were finally at the last stop. Relief came over Marie that now she'd be getting off the long train ride. It had been days since she had a decent bath.

"Are we here?" David looked up at her with those adorable big brown eyes. She gave him a reassuring smile.

"Yes, David. We are here. As soon as the conductor comes into our view I will ask him the name of the party sent to pick you up. Don't worry, I'll be by your side until they arrive."

"Okay."

She gave him a stern look. "David, you have to give your new family a chance, okay? Try to trust them."

"No one has ever wanted me before. I don't think they will either."

She noticed the conductor coming their way. "Sir? May I have a moment?"

He came forward with a smile. "I believe this is where the two of you get off. Will you need help with your bag, Miss?"

She shook her head. "No. I just have one small bag. However, can you give me the name of the party that is here to pick up David? Did Mr. MacFarley give you the name of the person to turn him over to?"

The conductor nodded, then reached into his coat pocket. He unfolded a small torn paper and scrunched his brows together. "It's hard to read. I believe he is going to be met by a Dr. Owen Gordon."

"What!" Marie almost jumped a foot in the air. How probable was it that Mr. Owen was ordering a mail-order bride *and* an orphan? "Are you sure?"

"That's what it says!" He handed the paper to her. "All I was told is that the man will have a red handkerchief sticking from his breast pocket."

Marie sucked in air. It was the same Mr. Owen! She looked down at the boy who was shaking. She was worried he was going to try to run away so she gave him a huge smile. "Are you ready to meet your new family?"

He shrugged. "If I have to."

Marie took his hand as they walked down the aisle of the train car and made their way carefully off the metal steps. The conductor was behind them since they were the last ones out.

"Ten minutes until the train leaves!" He cupped his hands around his mouth and repeated louder to make sure those standing on the deck heard him.

Marie and David walked towards the tall man standing by the ticket window. He was tall and quite handsome with dark hair and there it was, the red handkerchief.

She watched as a smile formed on his face as he stared at the boy. He looked at Marie but then his eyes went to the boy. He got down on one knee and David stopped in front of him and stared back. "Are you my new Father?"

"If you are from the orphan train, then yes, I believe I am."

David didn't say a word after that, but Marie knew he was trembling. His little hand in hers gave her all the indication that he was terrified. She understood.

"I'm Owen. Everyone calls me Doc Owen because I'm a doctor," he told the boy. "So if you don't feel like calling me Father yet, you can call me Doc Owen, okay?"

"Okay. Where are we going to live?"

"We are in Mill Ridge at the moment, but we'll be taking my buggy to Cooper's Ridge. It's a long drive from here but don't worry, I brought some provisions in case you are hungry."

"Are provisions food?"

"You bet they are. Would you like to tell me your name?" The doc was still kneeling down at eye level with David.

"It's David." He looked up at Marie. "She picked out my name because I remind her of King David. He was a King from long ago. In a place called Is-ra-el."

Doc Owen looked amused. "Is that so?"

David nodded.

"David, I'm going to speak with your escort right now. Would you like to take a ride in the buggy? It's right over there and you can climb up and wait for me, okay?"

"I can? Okay!" David made his way holding onto his small sack of clothes. He threw the bag in the buggy and it landed on the seat. Then he climbed up and sat in the back seat, looking so proud and happy.

It was a proud moment for Marie. She would miss the boy.

The doctor stood and held out his hand. "You must be the agent who escorted David here. Thank you for making sure he arrived safely."

"Your welcome. Mr. Owen, I have some bad news for you unfortunately and am not sure how to go about telling you."

"Bad news? About David?" His eyes looked so disappointed in that moment, she blurted out the whole horrible ordeal in one shot.

"No, no, no, sir! It isn't about David. Well, it will obviously affect him without a mother now. You see, I am not the boy's escort. My name is Marie Wilson and Dora Wilson is my step-sister. She is not coming, sir. She jilted you halfway here and ran off with a rich rancher and now you have no bride to take care of your new son. I am terribly sorry to have to bring you this awful news."

He shook his head, like he was trying to get cobwebs out of his ears. "You spoke so fast I hardly heard a word of your conversation, but it sounded like you said Dora was not coming to be my bride? Is this correct?"

She nodded, staring into his dark brown eyes. They were the same color as the boys. How interesting? No one would know the boy was an orphan. He had the same hair coloring, too. "I'm afraid so. Since she jilted you, I felt it was my duty to make the trip here to inform you of your loss. Luck having it, I found David along the way and wanted to make sure he got here safely since we were heading to the same destination." Although she didn't know at the time the child was going to be adopted by Doc Owen.

She thought he would be angry but instead she noticed a twinkle in his eye. He tilted his head and asked, "What are you doing for the next ten years?"

"What? I, uh, well, I haven't thought about it much!"

"I have an idea. Are you planning to go back to New York?"

She shook her head. "As of right now, I have nowhere to go. My original plans were to get Dora settled in Cooper's Ridge and find a job to support myself."

"A job? This is getting even better than I thought. Come on, let's go to Cooper's Ridge together. We can talk on the way."

"I, uh, it isn't proper, is it?"

Doc Owen shrugged. He leaned in and whispered in her ear. "Who cares. Are you ready?"

She followed him to the buggy where David was jumping up and down excitedly on the back seat. She set her carpet bag beside his feet as the doctor helped her onto the bench and climbed up beside her. He took the reins and they took off down the main street of Mill Ridge.

There were a lot of townsfolk out and about today. Doc Owen waved as people shouted his name and moved out of his way. He kept the horse going until they cleared the town. She hadn't said a word until now.

"I'm obliged for the ride to Cooper's Ridge, Doc Owen."

He gazed at her and gave her a huge grin. "Our first stop will be to see Pastor Murphy. He actually owns the town of Cooper's Ridge."

"We have to stop and say hello to him first? Since he owns the town that does make sense."

Doc Owen shook his head. "Not at all. But, he'll be the one to marry us."

Marie practically turned in her seat. "To what? Doc Owen, what are you thinking?"

He grinned. "Well, you said you didn't have anything to do for the next ten years, so, I figure you may as well take Dora's place since she done ran off and left me high and dry!"

"You want me to take Dora's place as your bride?" Was this man right in the head?

He nodded and grinned again. "Why not? You are obviously not going back to your family in New York. Dora wrote in one of her letters how your father beat her so I'm assuming he beat you as well. I'm sure you wish to stay far from that man."

"He did no such thing? Dora lied to you, sir! My father is a man of integrity. At least he was until he basically threw me away."

The doctor shook his head. His next words told her that he believed what she said. "I'm sorry to hear she lied. I'm glad she won't be the one to marry me. Makes sense to become my bride. I need a mother for David. I had this all planned out since my life has turned around here."

"Did you ever tell Dora you were taking in an orphan child?" Because Marie certainly hadn't read that in any of his letters.

"No. I was going to tell her when she got here in hopes that she wanted to be a mother. David was supposed to be here a few weeks ago, but he ran away from what I understand." Owen turned back to check on the boy. Luckily, David wasn't paying attention to their conversation. His little face was staring at the fields and acres and acres of ranch land, something those pretty brown eyes had never seen before. Some cows in the distance caught his attention and he was transfixed.

Marie looked from David to Owen. They were both as happy as birds in the sky. Doc Owen wasn't horrible to look at and David did need someone to care for him that understood how it felt to feel unwanted.

The last two years had been the worst years of her life. While her mother was alive, her father treated them both with respect and care. After her mother had died, their home had been cold and lonely until he met Constance and remarried. Well, Marie thought it would be warm and inviting once again with a new family. But, Constance and Dora had fooled her father. Maybe he even knew it and was not able to do anything about it. Or, he didn't want to. She wasn't sure.

Now she had the opportunity to build a family of her own. She could make it warm and inviting like her mother had done for her so many years ago.

She should ask him to stop the buggy right now and let her out. She didn't deserve this, did she? What if she messed it all up? After all, her step-mother had been good at telling her how horrible of a person she was even if Marie didn't believe her at first. But after a while, a person will start to believe what they are told. Maybe Marie got out just in time.

"I can't believe I'm going to say this," she told Doc Owen.

He gazed at her for a moment and she saw the hope in his eyes. "You can't turn back now," he said.

"I don't plan to. I think I'm going to marry you."

Chapter 6

Owen wanted to throw out the loudest *yeehaw* of his life but restrained himself. A smile crossed his face when she told him she was going to marry him. Her eyes slowly moved away as if she were shy. There was a slight blush on her cheeks. He wasn't sure if it was from the sun or from her embarrassment.

He didn't know what she had to be embarrassed about since marriage seemed like the logical thing to do. She was alone. The west was a cruel and heartless place, especially for a woman alone. He was alone and needed a bride. And she wasn't difficult to look at. She wore a simple woven skirt that had seen better days and a long-sleeved faded white blouse, along with a bonnet that tied under her chin. Her hair, the little that he could see, was pure blonde, and her eyes were blue. He had noticed her eyes the moment they met.

Doc Owen glanced at her carpet bag sitting on the floor of the back seat of the buggy. "Is that all you brought along?"

She stared at him, confused, then followed his eyes to the lonely carpet bag. She nodded, sadly. "My dresses were all given to my step-sister. I only have two changes of clothes with me."

"I've put some money back, knowing you may need things to live in Cooper's Ridge. You'll want to buy yourself material to make dresses unless you can find ready-made. The mercantile will have everything you may possibly need. There is also a small fabric shop in town."

"That's very kind of you, Doc Owen. However, I do have my own money. My father gave me money for the trip in case of an emergency."

Owen was good at reading people and decided she was holding back from telling him something important. Maybe she was afraid to tell him anything more, he was a stranger to her after all. Perhaps later down the road she will be honest. Right now, he wasn't going to take her word as the gospel truth. After all, her sister had lied and schemed her way until she found a better deal, then up and ran off.

"You keep the money your father gave you. It's best to have some money put back in case of an emergency like he said. I'll provide for my wife."

He noticed how her stiff shoulders relaxed when he told her that. Had she been worried she'd spend all her money for new dresses and then she'd be stuck without a dime to her name in case she wanted to run off at some point? He sighed. Perhaps he was thinking way too much. He had a son now who was a known runaway and was about to marry a woman he wasn't sure if she'd stay married or run away at a moments notice.

Owen wanted a family. Was this the family he had bargained for?

*****

It was a little over an hours ride to Cooper's Ridge. He gazed over at Miss Wilson to find her eyes drifting shut. She was leaning to the far side then she'd start leaning towards him. Owen wanted to place his arm around her shoulder and pull her to him so she could rest against his shoulder but thought better of that idea until they were married.

He hoped the pastor was at the church. Owen didn't want to put off the ceremony since she was a bit frightened even though she told him she'd marry him. A bride in flight was not what he wanted to bring to Cooper's Ridge. At least he had a bride to marry now and the boy would have a mother. Wasn't that all that mattered?

Owen glanced back to see the boy still wide awake, his eyes fixed on the ranch land. He pointed. "There's a cow. It's huge!"

"It's a bull, son. There are plenty out in the fields surrounding Cooper's Ridge. You'll have to be wary of them. Some can be downright mean."

"They do look mean. Is he going to chase us?" The boys voice rose.

"No. He isn't too bad, that one. You'll know when he's going to get mean. You'll hear him snorting out of his nostrils if you are too close. When you see that, you better get on home!" Owen didn't tell him there was a fence protecting the town from the bull. He wanted to make sure the boy didn't run away again. If he knew there was a mean bull close by, maybe it would keep him closer to home. He hoped, anyway.

"I'll just keep far away from him," the boy reasoned.

"You're a smart kid," Owen told him. "Keep those smarts and you'll grow up to be a great man."

"My goodness, I believe I dozed off." Miss Wilson blinked several times. "I'm sorry."

"Don't be sorry," he told her. "You've had a terribly long train ride here. I'm sure you're exhausted."

"It was truly not the adventure I thought traveling would be."

He gave her an understanding look. "You'll be able to sleep in a decent bed once we are married."

She didn't reply. When he turned to concentrate on keeping away from the drop-off close to a small bridge-like structure, he heard her gasp.

"Are we going to make it across?"

"Yes. It's sturdy, just narrow. Don't worry, I have everything under control."

Even so, she scooted closer to him until her shoulder was touching his. It felt nice. He wanted to touch her to let her know she had nothing to worry about but knew better than to take his hands off the reins over the gulch. Even though the horse went over this area hundreds of times in the last six months, he was never comfortable until the buggy was across the bridge.

"Sit tight," he told them then looked back to see David hanging over the side of the buggy. "David, sit down properly!"

The boy pulled back, a frightened look on his face. Was he that scared to be reprimanded? Had he been mistreated at the orphanage? David hadn't been afraid until Owen spoke up. Had Owen sounded too stern? Even so, it didn't hurt the boy to be a bit frightened since falling from the buggy and down into the gully would get him hurt, or even killed.

He was about to explain this to David, when Miss Wilson's voice sang out. "David, the reason you must sit still and away from the edge is so you don't fall out and tumble down that gully. I don't want anything to happen to you. Especially before we get home."

She had turned to the boy, still clinging onto the bench with one hand.

"I'm sorry," he told her. His bottom lip was sticking out, pouting in a way that Owen wasn't sure if he was truly sorry or trying to get her sympathy. Time would tell.

"We're over the gully," he told them. "You can both relax."

"Thank goodness." He caught a glimpse of her wiping her brow and letting out a sigh. It made Owen smile. When he gazed at her she was looking back at the road they just crossed over. "That can be quite dangerous. Will anyone ever fix the road?"

"I believe the town council committee has been talking about widening the road with a better bridge. Time will tell if and when it gets accomplished."

"I certainly hope so. Is this the only way to Cooper's Ridge?"

He nodded. "I'm afraid so. Don't worry, I'll make sure you always get across safely."

"Thank you."

"You're welcome. Cooper's Ridge really has everything we need, but once a month I have to travel to Dallas to pick up my supplies. I usually stay overnight since it takes a few hours to get there. You and the boy can come along."

She gave him a grateful look and smiled. "That will be nice."

"I usually have a nice meal at the hotel's restaurant. You'll probably want to walk downtown and see some of the shops. There are so many there."

"I haven't shopped in years, actually."

"Why not?"

She shrugged and stared straight ahead as they neared the town. The church stood out over the rest of the buildings, it's pointed roof sticking up higher than the rest of the buildings. "When my father remarried, I was not allowed to spend any of the household money or buy myself anything. My clothes were given to Dora and eventually I got removed from my bedroom into a small closet behind the kitchen."

Anger at the thought of his future wife being treated so badly raged through him. "Had this been going on in front of your father? How did he allow this to happen?"

She shook her head. "He was always working at the bank. Before he remarried, it was just the two of us. He'd come home at normal hours and we'd share supper together and talk. When he remarried, it wasn't long after that I was given extra chores and had to take my meals when I was done with my work. By then, my plate of food was cold and I had to eat in the kitchen. There were many times Dora lied about me and I was sent to my room without supper."

"Didn't your father notice you were not at the supper table?"

"Not so much. He was always fed lies by my step-mother and step-sister. They fabricated lies about me and it seemed as if I was always getting into trouble. My father believed his new wife and never questioned anything because he was so busy working extra hours at the bank to provide for us."

"I'm sorry you were treated so poorly."

She gave him a sad smile. "It's over. I never have to go back to that house again. After my mother passed away, things were different, never to be the same again. I wanted to leave so badly and strike it on my own, but I was working until late evening and there was no time to find a job to earn money. I realize now that even if I had time to work outside the home, my step-mother would've found a way to steal my earnings."

"Here we are." He did reach over this time and laid a hand on her sleeve, then looked into her beautiful blue eyes. "You are home now. No one here will treat you badly ever again."

His bride-to-be looked away shyly and smiled. Then she told him, "I didn't mean to tell you all of that. It's in the past and talking ill of my family is wrong."

He shook his head. "It's not wrong. I'm glad you told me." He stopped the buggy in front of the church while she looked over the town. David was bouncing in the back seat.

"Are we here? Is this Cooper's Ridge? Is this our new home?"

"Yes, David. You are going to bounce right off that seat if you don't settle down."

He tried to stop, but when Owen got down from the buggy, the boy was still bouncing. He shook his head. This didn't seem like a runaway orphan, more like a kid in a candy shop.

"I'll be right back. I want to check if the pastor is in the church." Owen went inside to find his friend praying at the front of the church. He was on his knees in front of the huge wooden cross. Owen stood quietly to wait for him to finish. He knew Cooper heard him come in. The man heard and saw everything around him.

When Cooper stood, he turned and nodded to Owen. "How was your trip to Mill Ridge?"

"It was a success."

"The boy?"

"In the back seat bouncing around like a toad hopping into a water hole."

The pastor laughed. "That's good news. How about your mail-order bride? Did she show up?"

Owen smiled. "The original mail-order bride ran off with some rich rancher in Kansas."

Cooper moved down the isle to stand beside him. "You don't say? Now what will you do? The orphan will need a mother."

Owen clapped Cooped on the shoulder. "I hope you have time for a quick ceremony, my friend. I've got a better deal. Dora Wilson's step-sister is going to become my bride."

"Her step-sister? How did this happen? You have some explaining to do before I marry you!"

They both laughed.

Owen headed towards the door. "They're waiting out in the buggy. I'm going to get them now. Marie Wilson was the escort of my bride-to-be so I asked her to marry me since the other one didn't show."

Cooper's jaw dropped. "She said yes?"

"She said yes. It was either marry me or get a job and earn enough money for a train ticket back home to an unhappy life. She decided to stay."

"I'm impressed. When you left here this morning, I was certain you were coming back empty handed. Go get your bride. I'll get my wife for a witness. Holler down the street for Tom. He's at the stable. He can also witness since I need two."

"You know darn well if I holler down the street every one that hears will be in this church for a wedding in less than ten minutes."

Cooper smiled and motioned for him to go. "A wedding needs guests," he mumbled.

When Owen opened the heavy church door, he blinked several times. There was already a crowd surrounding his buggy. David was leaning over the bench again, talking to another boy about his age. Miss Wilson was carrying on a cheery conversation with several ladies. Two men stood watching with their arms crossed.

Owen had planned to marry, get the two of them settled and then open the office for a few hours. Now, it looked like the whole town was going to be at his wedding and there would be food and merriment all afternoon. This was not how he planned the day.

Was this an indication of how married life was going to be?

Chapter 7

When several women approached the buggy, Marie smiled and said hello. One of them introduced herself as Cynthia Hamilton, then introduced the others. They all gave her genuine smiles and seemed pleasant enough so she introduced herself and David.

They talked away about the town and gave her advice when they found out she was here to marry the doctor. Marie had a feeling they already knew who she was and why she was here when they came up to the buggy. Even so, it was nice to know such lovely people were in this small town.

Marie had never been in a small town quite like this before. She was excited to go exploring once they got settled. David was hanging over the side of the bench talking to another boy his age. She wasn't going to reprimand him about not sitting properly on the bench since the buggy was at a standstill.

She was glad to see the church front door open and Mr. Gordon come through as he walked towards the buggy. She supposed the next step was to go inside and have the pastor marry them. Was she ready for this? Then she heard the boy's giggling and realized he needed a mother. He needed one who understood how lonely and frightened he was. She was sure there would be challenges with the boy.

She had a good mother who taught her well. It was her duty to pass that on to David. He had a hard life. The Lord's words in the Bible she read said to take care of orphans and widows. This would be her future and her calling. Having Mr. Gordon beside her as her husband would be a blessing.

Marie realized once they were married, she'd be able to call him Owen instead of Doc Owen like everyone else called him. It made her smile and when he held out his hand to help her from the buggy, her huge smile caused him to give her a big smile in return.

"We'll proceed to the church," he told her, helping her down. Next, he motioned for the boy to jump from the seat. David had no problem getting down. He leaped from the buggy and took Marie's hand. She gave it a squeeze.

"Where are we going first?"

She leaned down. "Doc Owen and I are going to be married in the church. Once we become husband and wife, you will become our son and we will become one big family."

"I never had a family before." He hesitated to walk along with her. She was worried it was too much for him in one day.

Marie swung around and picked him up. Even though he was too big to be held, she wanted to be eye level with him. She held him in her arms and stared into his brown eyes, so he'd understand how serious she was. "David, a family always talks about the things that are bothering them. I want you to know that if you are afraid or scared you can always talk to me, okay?"

He nodded.

"Are you afraid right now?"

He formed his lower lip into a pout and nodded.

"You don't have to be scared. This won't take long and then we will go to our new home."

"Promise?"

"Yes. I promise. Have I lied to you yet?"

He shook his head.

"Okay. Let's get this ceremony started!" She set him on the ground and took his hand. She wasn't going to let it go until they were in the church. David's moods sometimes went from so happy to nervous as a bird with a barn cat on his trail.

"How's the boy?" Owen asked in a hushed tone so the boy didn't hear.

"I'm not sure. He looks like he wants to take flight like a scared goose."

"I'll keep an eye out, too. Once he gets a good night's rest, I'm sure he'll feel better."

"The doctor knows best," she joked, even though she was so nervous. Marie was good at holding in emotions. She had learned over the years from experience with her step-family to never let them see how she really felt or they'd use it against her and make her life miserable.

Somehow, the good doctor already knew she was. "Don't be nervous," he told her. "This will be over soon and we can go to the sanctity of our home."

"Thank you. Your words make me feel better."

He pulled open the door and held it for her as she and young David went through. Owen came in behind her, along with the group that was lingering around the buggy and several more townsfolk. By the time they got to the front of the church, the pews were already halfway filled up.

Marie stood in the front of the church watching in amazement as more people flowed through the doors, every single face smiling away.

"I don't understand this," she told Owen, who stood beside her. "Where are these people coming from?"

"By the time the pastor begins, the whole town will be here. I'll admit I didn't want to scare you."

"You knew this would happen?" She was discouraged by his words.

He nodded. "It always does. If even one person knows something, by the time you blink your eyes twice, the whole town knows. I'm sorry."

She glanced around the church. "They all seem happy about the wedding ceremony."

"There's not too much that goes on in Cooper's Ridge unless the townsfolk make it happen. One little thing usually winds up to be a whole day of celebration!"

"I'm afraid David may not be up to much more celebrating." She pointed to him on the first pew, leaning back, his eyes closed.

"He's plum tuckered out."

Marie observed the way Owen watched the boy. At some point she had to disclose to him all of the things the boy had gone through. Not that it would be an excuse to cater to the boy, but hopefully give Owen an understanding of the behavior at times. She sighed and turned towards the front of the church.

The pastor finally arrived with a beautiful older woman in tow. "Miss Wilson, this is my wife, Catherine. She is usually my witness for ceremonies like this, but I see we have many in the congregation right now. Actually, it isn't surprising to see the whole town here."

"I've heard this happens a lot," Marie mentioned. She looked at Catherine. "It's a pleasure to meet you."

Catherine came forward and gave her a hug. "Welcome to Cooper's Ridge. I'll stop by once you are settled. I know how it's like to be bombarded by the townsfolk. Don't worry, it's a wonderful place to live."

"Thank you." She hoped Catherine was right. Marie wanted to make a go of this new life that was being gifted to her. She looked up at the cross, asking God to give her the strength to carry on. She was so tired. It was probably the long train ride and then the buggy ride here. Even though she got a cat nap, her body was truly exhausted.

"If everyone would please be seated, we will start the ceremony," Pastor Murphy announced.

The congregation fell silent.

Pastor Murphy began talking. Marie didn't really hear a word he said until he looked at her pointedly. "Marie Wilson, do you take Doctor Owen Gordon as your husband, in sickness and in health until death do you part?"

She glanced at Owen, who was watching her and nodded. "I do," she told him softly.

The pastor turned to Owen. "Do you, Owen Gordon, take Marie Wilson as your bride, to have and to hold, in sickness and in health until death do you part?"

Owen was still staring into her eyes. "I do."

She didn't realize he was holding her hands. When he tugged and brought her closer, she realized the pastor had told him to kiss the bride. How did she miss that? Probably because she was staring into his eyes and got lost in them. He came closer and gave her a soft kiss on the mouth to seal the marriage.

"I now present to you, Mr. and Mrs. Owen Gordon. Welcome to Cooper's Ridge!"

The congregation began to clap and cheer as Owen scooped up David on his hip and took her hand. He led her down the aisle as townsfolk yelled out from the crowd their congratulations.

"Festivities tonight at the saloon!" someone called out.

"Do we have to go to a saloon?"

"There's no alcohol there," Owen told her. "It is a place to eat and hold meetings. Cooper thought having alcohol will just be a temptation to those here who were trying to go down a straight and narrow path. Anyone who lives here knows it before signing a lease for their property."

"You'll have to tell me more about this town's history."

"I really don't know much more than that. We'll go on a tour soon, but we better get this little feller home. He's sleeping so sound he never jumped at the sound of the applause."

They put David in the front seat this time between them and drove the short distance to the doctor's office. It was a two story house with a large front porch that held several benches and chairs for patients while they waited to see the doctor.

Tom from the livery was walking towards them. "Want me to take care of the buggy, Doc?"

"Thank you, Tom."

Owen hopped down, picked up a sleeping David as Tom held out his hand for Marie. "Welcome to Cooper's Ridge, ma'am."

"Thank you, sir."

Tom jumped onto the seat and took off towards the livery at the end of the street. Marie followed Owen up the three steps to the porch and through the front door. He turned left into a parlor and set the boy on the small settee. Marie saw a blanket folded over one of the other chairs and placed it over the sleeping boy.

"We'll let him sleep there for now," Owen told her. "Let me show you around."

Marie followed Owen back out of the parlor into the entryway. Another door was directly across from where they stood. He turned the knob and went inside.

"Is this where you work?"

"It's my office. One of the biggest rooms in the house. The patients can wait outside or in the entryway. I placed a bench and a few chairs there also."

"You have quite a nice office."

"Thank you."

She followed him down the hall to a kitchen and dining area where a simple wooden table sat with four chairs, a cook stove, wash basin on another large table and shelves attached haphazardly to the walls with cooking utensils and pots and pans. There wasn't even a curtain on the window. A back door led to a nice size yard that was in need of weeding.

She looked around. There was a lot of work to be done, but it was nothing like at home. There, she toiled from sun-up to sundown to make others happy. This place would be her home and she'd make it cozy and a place to come home to when the doctor was done for the day.

"Would you care to see the upstairs?"

"Certainly. Let me get my carpetbag and I'll move it out of the way." They both went back down the hallway to the front door, where the two bags sat against the wall. She wondered what Owen thought of her scarce luggage? Both bags were tattered and worn. She picked up hers and Owen took the boys. He started up the stairs first.

Marie followed behind. On the second level were three doors down a hallway. Owen went into the first one at the top of the stairs. "This will be our room. Since we are married, I see no reason why we can't share the bed."

A slight dip in her pulse caused Marie to stumble with her carpetbag. Owen put out his arm to keep her from falling. The next thing she knew he had wrapped his arm around her as her knees buckled. "Are you all right?"

"Yes, I'm fine."

"It's been a long day for you. Why don't you lie down and rest. It will be a few hours before we are expected at the saloon."

"I believe I will. It's been a long, exciting day."

"Fortunately, I'm use to working long hours as a doctor. Sometimes, I've been known to go for two days at a time until all my patients are taken care of."

His words surprised her. "Now that you have someone to share the responsibilities with, those hours will have to change. You have a family now to care for."

"Yes, ma'am," he teased. "Please, rest a spell. I'll wake you early enough so you can wash up before we leave."

"Thank you. Now that we are married, may I call you Owen?"

He grinned. "Only if I may call you Marie."

"Of course." Marie motioned for him to go. "If you keep talking, I'll never get any rest."

He laughed as he went out the door, closing it softly behind.

Marie laid down on the large bed, wondering how marriage would be with him. Since her mother died, she never got to ask about weddings, or marriage or any of the things some of her schoolmates knew about. She heard everything second hand and always wished there was someone she could talk to. Ophelia was good to her but they never discussed the subject of marriage.

She closed her eyes. Then opened them wide and looked around the room. A sturdy wooden dresser with a huge mirror attached sat in the corner, while a wooden chair was tucked up beside the dresser. The rest of the room was bare except for two hooks on the one wall near the door. An oil lamp hung from a large iron hook beside the door.

Owen certainly lived a plain life. Would he be happy to know that Marie planned to decorate the house? If he was not willing to pay for some things, she'd have to use her own money. That was okay, she had no plans to go anywhere. This was going to be her life and her home.

Even so, there was a part of her money she had to hide away in case of an emergency. In case he didn't want her anymore and she had to flee on her own.

She always had a plan.

Chapter 8

A soft knock on the door woke Marie. The room was not as bright as earlier, and she gazed towards the window across the room. Light was starting to fade. Had she slept all afternoon? She scurried out of bed and opened the door to find David looking up at her with a huge smile on his face. "Doc Owen said it's time to wake up. He sent me on this important mission."

Marie kneeled down so she was eye level with him. "You did a very good job, David. I'm up and will be downstairs in less than ten minutes. I'm going to wash up and fix my hair."

"Okay. Promise?"

"Yes, David. I promise."

He reluctantly turned and started down the stairs.

"David?"

The boy turned to her, a frown on his face. "Yes?"

"You're safe here, okay?"

"Okay." Her words caused him to give her a weak smile. When she closed the door to wash up, Marie wondered why he was looking so sad. She threw in those last words in case he was feeling scared being in a strange place. Hopefully, time would make things better.

After she washed up, Marie took her hair down from the tight bun she always wore and brushed it out. It fell in soft waves across her shoulders and down her back. She loved how the curls always twisted without having to use any type of heating tool. Dora had straight hair and spent hours every night finger curling her hair and pinning it to her head. The next morning she spent nearly an hour unwrapping the pins to get the kind of curls Marie had naturally.

Actually, she was always ordered to help Dora with her hair. It took over an hour which usually made Marie miss breakfast before she was ordered to start another chore. Marie looked in the mirror, her blue eyes staring at her brushed hair. It was lovely. Dare she leave it down? She noticed at the church about half of the women wore their hair down, while others were put up in chignons.

Marie pulled out a clean faded flower patterned skirt from her bag that wasn't as tattered-looking as the one she wore here. She shook it a few times, then changed her skirt and put on a long-sleeve blouse that tucked into the waist of the skirt. She gave herself an appreciative nod in the mirror. She looked and felt clean and presentable. It gave her more confidence to meet all the people who would be present in the saloon.

When she got to the bottom of the stairs, Owen was helping David straighten out his shirt. He showed him how to tuck it into his pants and added a small bow-tie. When Owen turned he had also changed into fresh clothes. He looked even nicer than she remembered. "You both look extremely handsome this evening," she told them.

David's big brown eyes stared at her. "So do you!"

"Thank you," she said back, giving him a small curtsy.

Owen was staring as well.

"Are you okay, Owen?" Marie didn't understand why he didn't move yet.

"I'm, yes. I'm fine. You do look quite handsome, Marie. I like your hair down."

She shyly smiled back as he continued to watch her. "Thank you, Owen. Shall we go to the saloon?"

"We're going to a real saloon? Honestly?"

Owen and Marie both laughed. "Yes, David. Why are you so surprised?" Marie took his hand as Owen held the door open for the two of them.

"One of the orphans had a dime novel about an outlaw in the saloon and a shoot-out." He looked excited and a tiny bit terrified. "Will we see an outlaw? Will he shoot his guns like in the book?"

Marie squeezed his hand. "Of course not, David. Those are only stories. The saloon here doesn't even have alcohol that makes some men mean and do bad things."

"Why do they call it a saloon then?"

"I can't say, David. I really don't know. I think that Pastor Murphy wants this town to be different than other towns."

The boy nodded as if he understood but she really didn't think he did. For now, that was all the explanation he was going to get. As they walked down the street he turned towards the other people who were also heading towards the saloon, forgetting all about their conversation.

Owen leaned in. "Thank goodness he is distracted. I thought I'd have to jump in with an explanation to help you explain things here."

She smiled, thankful he was willing to do so. "Children do not want details."

"You are quite observant," he mentioned.

She gave him a smile. "I use to volunteer at The Children's Village with my mother. I learned children's behavior there. Some were good, others not so good. That was a long time ago."

"Perhaps your knowledge and experience will help us with David."

They both watched David's excitement the closer they got to the saloon. Music filtered from inside as others hung around the porch and by the swing doors of the entrance. Owen and Marie held onto an excited David as they entered.

Everyone inside began to clap.

"Here they are, the new couple. Congratulations, Doc Owen!" One man shouted over the crowd, then slapped Owen on the back. Her new husband shook hands and took it all in stride.

Marie watched as he spoke to each person who congratulated him. David stood between them, his little feet trying hard to stay still. She leaned down. "Would you like to go to the food table with me and get something to eat?"

"I do! I do!"

She laughed and motioned to Owen that they were heading to the table. He nodded in understanding even though every single man in the saloon was greeting him. It had to be a bit overwhelming for the doctor. Although, when she looked back, he seemed to be perfectly at ease.

Marie was happy to stay in the shadows as she helped David fill a plate. There were fresh rolls, a plate of meats and cheeses, bowls of fresh fruit, steaming pots of soup and chicken and dumplings and plenty of cakes that were making little David's mouth drool.

She leaned over with a handkerchief she extracted from inside her sleeve and wiped the corner of his mouth. "David, why don't we take our plates and sit along the far wall?"

He followed her and they sat between a young couple and one of the ladies who greeted them earlier at the wagon. The woman turned and smiled when Marie and David sat down.

"Hi Marie. It's me, Cynthia Anderson."

"Hello, Cynthia. You're married to the livery owner, is that right?"

Cynthia gave her a wide smile. "I sure am. Some day I'll tell you all about how he saved me from a horrible future."

At that moment, Marie didn't feel all alone in a crowd of people. "It's nice to hear someone else had a life they had to get away from. I hope that doesn't offend you."

"Not at all, Marie. Congratulations on your marriage, by the way."

"Thank you. You've met our son, David, this morning at the wagon. He's very excited about being in a saloon. He thought there would be an outlaw in here and he'd get to witness a shoot out."

The two ladies laughed. "I'm afraid Paster Murphy would never allow that, but, sometime soon we'll talk about outlaws and gunfights. My husband has seen quite a few in his life before he moved here and started taking care of the horses."

"He did?" Her words caught David's attention. He stared at her, those adorable brown eyes so wide. "Did he shoot an outlaw?"

"I'm afraid he *was* an outlaw. Until Paster Murphy helped him see the light. Now he's a good man."

"I can't wait to meet him. Is he here?"

"He'll be along shortly and I'll introduce the two of you."

"Marie, can I go get a cookie?"

"Go on. Make sure you come right back here and don't go outside without Owen or I, okay?"

"Okay." The boy scooted off his chair and darted between a few others to make his way to the food tables.

"He's a sweet boy."

Marie raised a brow. "He is very sweet. He is also an orphan who ran away a few times before he finally got here. We'll have to be careful until he feels comfortable enough with his new family."

"I'm sure he'll be fine now that he's finally here." Cynthia waved to someone. "There's my Tom!"

Tom was a tall man, with an authoritative walk that had others turning to watch as he made his way towards his wife. Marie was quite shocked when Cynthia stood and wrapped her arms around his neck and he pulled her to him and gave her a hard kiss in front of the whole saloon. Marie had to admit she was just as intrigued along with everyone else at their brass behavior.

"Darling, I'm so happy you are here early. How did you manage?"

He gave her another peck on the cheek. "Sam came in early. She doesn't want to come to the party so she said she'd take over so we can do some dancing tonight."

"I'll have to thank her when I see her next," Cynthia told her husband.

Tom walked her to the chair and told her to sit and wait on him. He tipped his hat to Marie. "Ma'am." Then he turned back to his wife. "I'll be right back. First, I want to congratulate the groom and then I want you all to my self." The man strutted away, knowing full well there were more eyes on him than his wife alone.

"Isn't he the most handsome man you've ever seen? Oh, I'm sorry. Of course, Doc Owen would be your handsome man! I can't wait to tell you all about my husband. We should have tea together soon."

"I'd like that." Marie had no friends left when she lived in New York. There was never time to make any new friends either. The ones she had before her step-family came had all moved on after Marie kept thwarting their requests to visit. She had never wanted any of her old friends to see how she had to live.

That was all over with now. She had a new life and a new husband and child. How had this happened so fast?

Marie was so afraid it was all a dream and she'd wake up tomorrow in the closet behind the kitchen.

*****

When Owen looked over to see where Marie was, he realized she had a panicked look on her face. The other woman, Cynthia Anderson, was talking away and pointing to Tom, who stood in the group that surrounded him. Owen was no longer interested in speaking with the others. All he wanted to do was make sure Marie was fine.

"If you'll excuse me, my wife is patiently waiting for me."

One of the men laughed. "Would you listen to the doc, he's hen-pecked already."

Owen shook his head, a grin on his face. It didn't matter what they said. All he knew was Marie was new here and he needed to be by her side. She was quite pale and he hoped Anderson's wife wasn't telling her something to scare her. After all, Cooper's Ridge was a town filled with old outlaws who had redeemed themselves. That was enough to scare anyone. Especially a fragile human being from the east.

Cynthia looked up and gave him a great smile when Owen made his way to his wife, but he only had eyes for Marie. "Hello, Mrs. Anderson." He acknowledged Cynthia and turned to his wife. "Marie, is this night too much for you?"

"Not at all. David is having so much fun. I believe he found a few boys to talk to. Look over there." He hadn't come right back after he got a cookie. Instead, he was distracted by a few young boys he met. She'd have to teach him to listen to directions and always ask. But, not tonight.

She pointed to the group of boys. Owen turned and nodded his head in approval. "Good. Hopefully, that will keep him busy so I can have a dance with my wife when the music starts again."

She giggled. "I would be honored to dance with my new husband," she told him.

"Tom is waving for me." Cynthia stood. "Thanks for talking to me, Marie. We'll get together soon, I promise."

Marie waved to her just as soft music came from a group of musicians on a small stage at the far end of the saloon. Owen held out his hand. "Would you care to dance, Mrs. Gordon?"

"It would be my pleasure." She took his hand as he led her to the floor. Her small hand was warm and fit perfectly in his. It had been a long time since he danced with anyone. As the musicians played, others moved to the dance floor as well. As the two of them made their way around the dance floor, the others moved out of the way, still shouting out congratulations to the new couple.

Owen was enjoying the slow dance with his new wife, even if some were heckling them. He shook his head and kept apologizing, but began to laugh along with Marie when someone called out a silly remark about the new bride and groom. At least she was light-hearted and didn't get upset.

When the song came to an end, Marie raised her beautiful, bright blue eyes to his. He hoped and prayed she'd continue to look at him like she was doing now every single day.

Even though he knew he had killed that man in self-defense, the worry that she'd think of him as a horrible killer kept eating away at him. Cooper told him sometimes things were better left unsaid. He wasn't a murderer. He knew that as the truth, but wondered if Marie would be as understanding, too.

He knew he had to explain what happened sooner or later. When she found out, would she forgive him or look upon him like others did in his old hometown?

Only time would tell.

Chapter 9

Four months later

"David? Don't be in such a hurry. You almost forgot your lunch pail." She picked it up from the kitchen table and handed it to him. He grinned sheepishly as he grabbed it, then hurried towards the front door. She knew he wanted to catch up with his friends and walk to school with them.

He stopped, turned and ran back to her, grabbing her skirt with one arm and giving Marie a hug. "Thank you. Bye, Marie."

"Have a good day and listen to the teacher." She ruffled his hair as she spoke. Marie wondered when he'd call her Mother, but she decided from the start she would not push him to say something he wasn't ready to say. He'd already been let down by so many adults in his short life. Plus, he was quite jumpy at times. She was afraid that he'd run away if he became too upset. It was a fine line they walked each day.

Hopefully by now, he had to realize they were his family and this was his home. No one would ever interfere. Owen and Marie both made a vow together one evening as they talked about their future together as his parents.

She stood on the front porch watching as he caught up with Marcus and Johnny. The three of them took their time walking towards the church where school was being taught until the new building was finished. It was a fine sight to see that he had made some friends.

According to Cynthia, the new teacher had been stuck at a place called Christmas Inn during a winter snowstorm in Kansas. The teacher showed up in Cooper's Ridge after the snow melted, along with her husband, Harrison, who opened a gunsmith shop.

Marie had met her the day she took David for his first day of school. Miss Molly seemed very lovely and yet Marie had a feeling she would be quite strict when it came to matters of importance.

"Good morning to you, Marie." Cynthia waved, then managed her way up the three steps, whipped her skirts past Marie along with her basket of goods.

"What do you have today?" Marie asked her new friend, trying to peek under the cover.

"Eggs. I hope you are in need."

Marie held the door open for her to go through. "We haven't been paid in eggs this week yet. Although, that may change depending on what patients Owen has today."

"Do I smell coffee?"

"Of course. Follow the aroma straight to the kitchen, Cynthia. I have the pot simmering on the stove."

"Let me help," she insisted, setting the basket on the table and picking up the handle with a thick cloth. Cynthia poured them each a cup and set them down on the table. After adding some cream, they sat at the table for their usual long morning conversation.

"Tom wants a child."

"Oh? What about you, Cynthia. Do you?"

She nodded, then closed her eyes. "I do. Except I want all of Tom's attention. He treats me like a princess and it's so indulging that I'll be honest and say I don't want to give that up when a baby comes along even though it's what I'm supposed to do. Am I rotten to the core for feeling so selfish?"

Marie laughed. "You are the least selfish person in this town, Cynthia."

"You didn't know me before Tom married me. I was a terrible person."

Marie was concerned for her friend. She took Cynthia's hand. "You told me your family was not kind to you. I do understand how you felt. I have a stepmother who wanted me out of the house so badly she forced me to escort my horrible stepsister here."

Cynthia's eyes grew wild. "You haven't told me this story. Go on, my dear. I want every detail."

Marie spent the next ten minutes giving Cynthia explicit detail of her life in New York City. When she was finished, Cynthia took her hand and squeezed it. "We both have had hateful people in our pasts. I think it's time we get beyond that and live our lives the way God intended us to. Here in this growing town with the loves of our lives. We have a purpose to fulfill in Cooper's Ridge."

Cynthia's words were wise and she wanted to leave the hurts behind even though she did miss her father and Ophelia. Marie made a note to herself to pen them both a letter soon. There was something else on her mind. She wondered if it was permissible to speak of private affairs? Then she told herself Cynthia was the perfect person to help her deal with any situation of the heart.

"Owen didn't choose me to be his wife. He had no other choice when my sister ran off with someone else." There, she said what had been in the back of her mind for a while now.

Cynthia shook her head. "You don't see what I see at all, do you?"

When Marie just stared at her, Cynthia began to pat her hand. "You are so naive, my dear and I mean that sincerely. Maybe even more than I ever was. Doc Owen adores you. I can see his eyes follow you around a room even when he is busy speaking with someone else. I saw it the day you two married."

"Truly?" Marie had the impression he was doing his duty, marrying her for David's sake. Which is what they originally agreed upon and yet she was starting to want more out of this marriage of convenience.

Cynthia gave her a long stare, then her mouth moved into an all-knowing smile. "You haven't consummated the marriage yet, have you, dear?"

How did she tell Cynthia that by the time Owen came to bed, she was already under the covers with her eyes closed, pretending to be asleep. She had often felt his body weight as he climbed into his side, but he never bothered with more than a kiss since the day she came here. Now that they were man and wife, she knew he had the right to consummate and yet he hadn't made any effort at all. Was she not enticing enough for him? Her stepsister often told her she'd never catch a man with her frumpy looks.

"Your silence tells me the truth of the matter."

Marie sighed. "I'm not comfortable speaking these things out loud."

Cynthia laughed and leaned over, her voice softer than normal. "Oh, dear Marie. Wait until it happens. You will be spending the better part of the morning telling me how wonderful your husband is."

"I highly doubt it," she told Cynthia. When she saw the sparkle in Cynthia's eyes, Marie felt a wave of jealousy wash over her. She tilted her head. "Are you serious?"

Cynthia nodded, then closed her eyes and breathed in deeply. "It's wonderful even though they tell you it's a horrible duty that a woman has to put up with. I've been keeping it all inside, since we barely know each other, but now that it's all in the open, here's what you can expect."

The next ten minutes had Marie blushing and sucking in her breath. At one point she held her hands over her ears. "That's enough, Cynthia. This can't be for real!"

Cynthia stood when she heard the front door open and close. "I have to go. I believe your husband is coming down the hall right now." She gave Marie a hug and laughed out loud. "I promise if you look at your husband when you are speaking you will see the truth in his eyes."

"Good morning, ladies." Owen was always polite to everyone. He gave Cynthia a smile and walked her to the door when she mentioned she was just leaving.

"Have Tom stop by this week. He mentioned his shoulder was still bothering him. I'd like to take a look."

Cynthia agreed as she went out the door. Marie was grateful her friend left as her husband entered the kitchen. She hoped and prayed her face wasn't the color of crimson as she silently asked God to forgive her for listening to such things. Even if she was guilty for wondering if things like that really happened between a man and a woman or if Cynthia was trying to shock her.

Her friend was quite outspoken and a bit more vivid than some folks in town were able to stomach. In these past few months, Marie had grown to love the visits between them. She didn't care what others thought of Cynthia, although she didn't want Owen's reputation as a fine doctor impaired by her friendship. If that happened, she was sure Owen would take her side.

Wouldn't he? Did he care enough about her to defend her if someone thought Cynthia wasn't appropriate company for a doctor's wife?

"Marie? What are you thinking about so intently that you can't answer me?" He was smiling and yet there was a slight crease on his forehead. He seemed concerned.

She always tried to be as honest as possible and speak her mind. "I was wondering when the townsfolk will complain about Cynthia's visits here. There are a few women who speak quite negative about her. I've heard whispers in church when she enters."

He sat in the empty chair, then took her hand. Marie kept her eyes lowered as she watched him take her hands in his. It was nice. Then she remembered Cynthia's words and looked up to see if he was indeed watching her.

She swallowed when he stared right into her eyes as if she were very important to him. It almost took her breath away. "Marie. Do you enjoy Cynthia's company?"

"Yes. It's nice to have a friend here." She felt her cheeks getting warm at the thought of their earlier conversation and tried hard to keep a solemn face.

He squeezed her hands and pulled them to him. "Then be her friend and tell those old biddies to mind their business." He leaned forward and placed a sweet kiss on her forehead. She sighed. He was such a wonderful, proper husband. She couldn't imagine him being any more of a gentleman than he was at that moment.

"You wouldn't mind if I call them out when they are saying ugly things? I was trying to be mindful of your business and position here, but I really wanted to give them a what for!"

He laughed. "Don't give it another thought."

She stood up when he did, then stood on the tips of her toes and give him a peck on the chin. "Thank you."

He pulled her close and returned the kiss, only this time it was placed on her mouth. He pulled back quickly. "Would you like to ride along with me to visit a few farms this morning?"

He had never asked her to go along before. "Don't you have office hours today?"

Owen shook his head. "Tonight. I'll have to eat a fast supper and open back up. Most townsfolk know I have to visit the farms each month. I pinned a note on the front door already so everyone is alerted. If there's an emergency this afternoon, they'll know where to find me."

Her husband had everything under control. "I'd love to ride along with you and see what you do." They didn't have farms in New York City. She wished David could come along but he had school. It was important for him to learn.

"Give me about thirty minutes to take care of some business in my office and we'll be on our way." He moved to his office and closed the door.

Marie was overly excited. She cleaned up the kitchen, washed the few dishes they made dirty and put away the eggs on a shelf above the cook stove. Then she went upstairs to find footwear. If she were going to a farm, she'd need her kid boots. After taking off the flat ballerina slippers she wore around the house, she pulled on her kid boots and laced each one up.

During the first week she was here, Marie had done some shopping at the local mercantile and one of the dress shops spending more than she had planned. Owen didn't know she used some of her savings, even though he forbade her to do so.

She had wanted the ballerina slippers so badly she bought them on a whim. David was with her at the time and the moment they returned home, he told Owen everything she bought.

Owen had glanced at her, knowing she had spent more than he gave her. Then he smiled and never said another word. She had been so relieved that day. She didn't want someone to constantly hover over her, making decisions even though he had the right to.

As she went back down to wait on him, she was thinking how perfect Owen was. His smile was so warm and welcoming and to be honest, it made her heart feel alive inside. For so long she was suppressed by a terrible woman and her daughter. Marie felt rejected by her own father and her mother was long gone. Ophelia was the only one who made her feel loved.

She missed the older woman and vowed this evening to write a long letter to her. Maybe she'd have time to pen one to her father as well. Sadly, she didn't miss home.

"There you are daydreaming again," her husband's gentle voice said beside her. She turned and almost bumped into his chest. He steadied her with his hand.

"I'm sorry. I was thinking about my father and Ophelia."

"You mentioned Ophelia before. I'm sure you miss her terribly. Why don't you invite your father and Ophelia to visit?"

She shook her head. "There's no way he'd come anyway. His new wife is bleeding him dry. She likes all the newest fashions and spends more than he can earn. Why do you think I'm here? He couldn't afford to feed all of us."

He held out his arm when they reached the porch, helping her down the steps she was able to go down on her own. He was always so gentle with her. "My offer stands. We have extra room here if any of your family would like to visit. If that doesn't suit, I'll pay for a room at the boarding house."

"You are so generous, Owen. Thank you. However, I doubt my father would visit." She didn't want his wife under her roof. Sadly, she'd make the offer but would prefer if they stayed at the boarding house. There was no need to tell Owen right now since she doubted he'd ever show up.

They walked towards the stable where her husband's buggy was kept. "Do you mind if I cross the street to let David's teacher know we'll be out of town? Just in case?"

He grinned. "You are a good mother."

She blushed. "Thank you. I try to do the best I can."

"Spoken like a woman who loves her son."

"I hope someday he calls me mother," she told him softly.

"He'll come around. It hasn't been easy for the boy until now. One day mother will pop out of his mouth like the most natural word in the world. Just wait and see. Go on now, I'll bring the buggy to the church."

"I hope so." She crossed the street and waved at Johnny's mother who was coming down the street waving to her.

"Marie? I was coming to see you. Johnny wanted me to stop by this morning and ask permission for David to have a sleep over. Marcus's mother already gave permission."

"What? The three boys having a sleep over? David has never been away from home since we arrived here." Marie wanted to say no right away. What if the boy got upset or scared and tried to run away. The look on her face must've shown.

"Are you well, Marie? You look pale."

Johnny's mother didn't know that David had run away many times. If he was going to be in her care, Marie had to be honest with her. "I'm worried, Evelyn. If David gets upset or scared, he might try to run away. He had done this several times on the orphan train and at the orphanage."

"Oh, dear. How rude of me to mention this to have you live those memories over and over. Don't worry, the boys will be together and I won't allow them to stay out past dark. You have my word."

She trusted Evelyn and the woman seemed responsible. She wondered if David wanted to stay? Of course, he wanted to be with his friends, and yet she had to be sure. "I'm going to the local farms to help Doc Owen with his visits. Would you mind if David comes to your house right away after school since I'm not sure we'll be back in time?"

"Of course. Stop by when you get back and you'll see for yourself David will be just fine. After all, your house is almost directly across the street from ours. If he seems upset, I'll bring him home right away."

By the time the buggy pulled up, Marie's heart had calmed down. She climbed on the seat before Owen reached out to help her. "Is there something wrong with David?" He had that concerned look on his face.

"David is fine. It's me who is having heart palpitations."

"You're in good hands, if you want my professional opinion," he told her, trying to put her at ease. "Truly, are you ill?"

She turned to him. "I'm scared out of my wits, Owen. David wants to spend the night at Johnny's house. The three boys will be having a sleep over. I'm worried he may get scared and run away."

Owen's eyes lit up. "We'll be alone?"

"Well, yes. David will be across the street at Johnny's house." Hadn't he heard her?

"Good."

"You don't mind then?"

Owen laid his hand over hers. He turned and stared into her eyes. "I don't mind at all. It's time the boys have some fun."

"The boys? We only have one."

Owen grinned, then whipped the reins to get the horse moving. As they left town the grin on his face got wider. He gazed at her a few times, still smiling. "Maybe it's time we think about having another son."

Her eyes got huge and she turned away almost gasping for air. The heart palpitations began pumping blood through her. She was overwhelmed with emotions. Oh dear, oh dear! Was he insinuating they do the things Cynthia had spoken of?

Chapter 10

Owen cracked the reins harder than he intended as they made their way out of town. It had been so hard these past few months having to be careful and stay far enough away from Marie. He knew he had the right as her husband to consummate their marriage and yet he was trying hard to be respectful. Still, she didn't seem too interested.

When she came to Cooper's Ridge, it wasn't to marry. She had no expectations of becoming a bride when she left her home. He realized he had to ease her into trusting him.

Now, he wanted to make her his true wife. When she mentioned David would be at the neighbor's overnight, he planned to bring the subject up in a way that she'd either say yes or no. At least then he'd know if she was interested in making this a real marriage.

Beside, it truly was time David had a sibling. The thought made him smile. He'd be a good big brother.

"Now I see you smiling in a way that makes me wonder why?"

Her soft voice caught him off guard. The question as well. A moment before she had blushed so hard her cheeks were a bright pink. "I was thinking of David and the possibility that he could have a brother or sister some day."

"Perhaps," she told him softly.

The knot in his chest tightened . Owen wanted to grab his hat and throw it in the air. He was pretty sure she just agreed to become his wife completely. He could barely take a breath so he pushed out air through his nose.

She giggled.

He turned to her. "What did I say?"

She shook her head and laid a hand on his arm. He was holding the reins tighter than normal. "Let's change the subject, please. Is the farm ahead the one we are going to?"

He gave her a smile, nodded and then winked at her. Then, he rolled his eyes for winking like a school kid and burst out laughing.

So did she.

It had to be their nerves. When he looked over at her, Marie was holding her stomach and shaking her shoulders so hard he thought at first she was upset until she raised her chin to look up into the sky and began laughing out loud.

He raised a hand and gently ran the back of his fingers across her cheek. She closed her eyes, then moved away, unsure and shy all of a sudden.

Owen thought she was the most beautiful woman he had ever laid eyes on. But there was a time and place for everything and he had work to do.

At the farm, he drove the buggy down a bumpy lane towards a barn in the distance, waved at the old man sitting in a rocker on the porch of a white-washed farmhouse and came to a stop under a huge oak tree.

Owen quickly jumped from the seat, came around to the other side and reached for Marie's hand. She allowed him to help her down and he grabbed his black doctor's bag. When he looked up old man McGarvey was slowly making his way off the porch. It'd be another ten minutes until he walked to the barn. "Let's go ahead inside and get started. Mr. McGarvey takes his good old time. I'll be done by the time he gets here."

"He looks very old," Marie commented. She followed him inside where one of the cows were walking around a stall.

"He's old as dirt, but he takes good care of his stock. This girl here is Elizabeth, named after the Queen of England. I won't say any more since the old man will tell you all about her in a detailed story. I'm doing a check-up on her to make sure the calf is still breathing and healthy."

"Can I help?"

Her words surprised him. "I'm not going to say no. Let's step inside and close the door so she can't get out."

Marie was good at following directions. She was careful not to get in the way but wanted to get closer to Elizabeth and pet her. He saw how badly she wanted to reassure the cow. "It looks like you have a soft spot for animals."

She nodded, then reached her hand out to pet Elizabeth's neck. "I love animals. By the way, I was wondering if we can have a dog? I think it would be good for David."

He wanted to say no, but how in the world did he refuse anything she asked for? "How about we discuss it over supper tonight? Since David won't be home we can stop and get something to eat at the café."

"The thought of not cooking sounds lovely."

Now Owen was worried that she was tired of taking care of him. "Do you enjoy cooking, Marie?"

She glanced over at him, then her eyes went back to the cow when it yelped. "Of course. I love cooking, but once in a while it's nice not to. Is Elizabeth all right? She seems distressed."

"She is having a calf and going through birthing pains, Marie." From the time he met Marie, she never once lied to him so he knew she wasn't saying she loved to cook to please him. She had been up front and honest with him every step of the way since they met.

Which made it easier to tell her what had been on his mind for days now. It was time he told her about his past. No matter that he was defending himself, he still killed someone. He had to get it off his chest. Before they got too serious, he wanted to know if she was capable of loving a man who shot someone dead. As a doctor it was his duty to save lives, not take them. He was an outlaw in every sense of the word.

That's all he wanted. Peace in his life, a town that believed in him and didn't judge and a good woman who loves him despite his flaws. He'd make it a point to talk about it after supper. He had to tell her and tonight was the perfect time since David wasn't home. Owen didn't think she was the type of woman who'd tolerate a man lying. Especially if there was a possibility that past may catch up to him.

Because it might. It just might.

*****

"Thank you for taking me along. I had a wonderful time and learned so much." Owen glanced at Marie. Her hair was a bit askew as she religiously pushed a few loose strands away from her face. Her cheeks were pink from running after a small litter of puppies at the last farm.

"You're welcome. It was a pleasure to have you ride along with me today. I hope we can do this more often."

"I sure hope so." She picked the puppy up and it licked her chin. She giggled. "Do you think David will want him?"

Owen grinned. "If he doesn't I'm sure you will. I think that little one has taken to you and I sure don't blame him."

Marie blushed again and looked away, settling the puppy in her lap. The little mouth opened wide and yawned, then snuggled up into a little ball. The ride back to Cooper's Ridge was slow and enjoyable. It had been a long day. He watched as Marie yawned more than once behind her hand. She was trying not to be too obvious.

"Maybe we'll rest a bit before going out to supper. I have some work to do after I drop the buggy off."

She agreed. "Sure. I'll take the puppy to the school. I'm sure all of the kids will want to pet him."

Owen didn't like that idea. "Maybe we should wait on that. The puppy should get used to us first before we introduce it to a crowd of children."

Marie tilted her head as if she were considering, then nodded. "I believe you have a good point. While you work, I'll find a nice crate for this little fellow to sleep in."

Owen dropped Marie and the puppy at the front door of their house, then went straight to the livery. Tom wasn't there. In his place was the young woman who wore men's pants so brazenly and worked for Tom. "Hey, there, Sam! Would you mind taking the buggy?"

"Hi Doc. Sure thing. I heard you got a puppy."

Owen was indeed surprised. They just rode into town. No one could possibly notice the little bundle Marie carried in the house that fast. "How did you know?"

She laughed. "Tom had to drop off some wheels at the same farm you were at earlier. He said your bride was chasing a passel of puppies around the yard and you were staring at her so hard you never noticed him passing by. He got back about five minutes ago."

How had he missed Tom? Now he felt foolish. Then he laughed. It was too late to worry now. "I'm sure he behaved in the same way when he married Cynthia."

"You men are too obvious. I'm never going to marry and look all starry-eyed like that."

Owen shook his head. "Never say never."

"Never. I don't want no part of that nonsense. Nope. Not for me. I'm perfectly happy right here, shoveling stalls and living my life just fine. And books. I plan to own a book store one day. That's all I need."

Tom strolled in, hearing the last of the conversation. "I told her one of these days she'll fall head over heels with one of those handsome cowboys she reads about in those silly books of hers."

Sam turned, hands on her hips. "I told you reading is not nonsense. I probably have more knowledge in my head than you'll ever have common sense."

He walked past her, laughing.

Sam made a face.

Owen left the stable in a better mood. There was nothing quiet about that young woman, but Tom had taken her under his wing. He supposed she'd grow up and find a man and settle down someday, have a family and be grateful for that like most women did, wouldn't she?

Sam had declared from the first day she got here she was never going to marry or let any man tell her what to do. Owen was interested to see how that would work out for her. Only time would tell. No matter, he had his own issues to deal with today.

He stopped in front of the church and stared at the steeple for a moment. Was he doing the right thing putting his past on the line wanting to tell his wife what happened before he came here?

"Come on in, Owen. It looks like you have something on your mind."

"Cooper? Do you stand by the door all day to see who passes by?" He started towards the front door of the church.

Cooper laughed. "I was actually getting ready to leave when I noticed you out here."

Owen followed him inside. They sat on the last pew towards the back of the church. Owen got right to the point. "I'm going to tell my bride what happened."

"It's probably best you do," Cooper told him.

That surprised Owen. Hadn't he always said it's better to leave the past alone? "Why the change of heart? You're the last person I thought would agree with me."

"I was actually coming to see you." He pulled a small folded square from his breast pocket and handed it to Owen.

When he opened the letter, his worst fear was staring him dead in the face. "I was terrified something like this may happen some day. I was a fool to think I could live a normal life. The day I killed Charlie Townsly was the beginning of the end for me. May as well put a bullet in me, too."

"It's not your fault. The man was going to kill you and take everything he could from the apothecary. He knew you had opium and other drugs in the office. He would've killed you."

"His brother doesn't think so. All he knows is I killed his only kin."

"After you told me about the threats his brother made from the jail house window, I kept a close eye on things there. I know how these men operate. When he was sent away to one of the prisons I'm familiar with through our ministry, I got word of the break-out. This gives you plenty of time to prepare."

Owen closed his eyes. "I have a wife and a son now I just put in danger."

Cooper laid a hand on his arm. "Owen. She gave vows to God to stand by your side. Don't you remember?"

"Of course I do. I know that, but I can't put her or David in harms way."

"You won't have to. There will be a showdown, Owen."

"Then I best pack up and be out of here by morning." The thought of leaving everything here crushed his heart. Would he have to run for the rest of his life? He had said from the time he killed Charlie, that he was an outlaw because he killed a man.

Now that the truth was slapping him in the face, Owen realized he was not an outlaw. Mostly, he was desperate to keep his family far from Charlie Townsly's brother, a real nasty outlaw who would gun him down or shoot him in the back. The night he shot Charlie, Owen had no idea who he was. All he wanted to do was defend himself and keep the man from robbing him of medicines that other sick people needed.

He stood. "I won't cause anyone else to lose their life."

Cooper stood and faced Owen. "When I said you had time to prepare, I meant right here. In Cooper's Ridge."

"I don't understand."

"Owen. This is your home."

"I thought it was, too. I don't want to leave here, and I'm not afraid to face Charlie's brother even though he'd probably kill me. I'm not a gun fighter. The fact is, I won't put the woman I love or my new son in harm's way. If I leave, at least they'll be safe."

Cooper shook his head and clamped down on Owen's shoulder. "If you weren't the doctor of this town, I'd throw you out of here for being such an idiot."

"You don't understand. I won't allow my family to come to harm."

Cooper laughed. "Neither will we, Owen. It's time you learn something when it comes to real friends. You're not going anywhere. This town will back you. It's why I built Cooper's Ridge."

Chapter 11

Something was bothering Owen. It didn't bode well with her how he constantly looked over his shoulder when they left the house. Besides that, instead of going to the café, they walked in the opposite direction.

"We aren't going to the café this evening?"

Owen looked over and grinned. "I got us the best place in the whole town for supper. Since the saloon is closed for the evening, Cooper is having our supper made right now. We'll have the whole dining area to ourselves."

Was this why he was so nervous? She decided not to borrow trouble and smiled back. "For a moment I thought something terrible was about to happen. I'm so relieved. How nice of Pastor Murphy to open up the saloon for us. But, why would he do that?"

When Owen seemed to hear but didn't answer, she became concerned again. There was something in the air tonight and Marie wasn't able to pinpoint what. Ever since he had come back from the stable earlier, he seemed distant. Was she borrowing trouble?

Earlier, Marie had made lemonade and knocked softly on the door knowing he had work to do. He never answered even though she heard him shuffling papers She wanted to open the door to make sure he was okay. Instead, she announced that she'd leave the glass by the table outside the room.

Then, she had gone up to their room to freshen up. There was mud on the hem of her skirt and she wanted to look nice for supper with him this evening. Marie had almost forgotten about Ophelia's gift to her. She pulled it from the carpet bag and tore open the wrapping to find a beautiful cream blouse, along with a flowered skirt and light shawl to match. It was perfect for tonight's outing.

Now, all dressed up and feeling quite lovely, she was surprised when Owen never mentioned her new clothes and she didn't think it was polite to mention them herself. She noticed his arm was quite stiff as she held on to it. He was tense and upset. She stopped. "Owen? What's wrong?"

They stood in the street staring at each other. He let out a huge sigh. "Let's go inside the saloon so we can talk."

"I think I'd prefer to know right now before we go inside."

He looked around, which concerned her, then said. "The streets aren't really too safe right now for us. We need to go inside."

"What? This town is not dangerous? What are you talking about?" She was more confused than ever.

Owen wrapped his arm around her shoulder and began to move them towards the saloon doors. "I'll explain everything once we're inside."

A chill crept up Marie's spine. She complied and went along inside the saloon, now more worried than ever. The room glowed softly from a few candles set here and there and one of the round tables was covered with a white cloth. The table, set for two, had a bright candle that flickered in the center. A few oil lamps were also lit to lead the way towards that table.

Owen had told her when she first came here the saloon wasn't used for drinking, but for a meeting place with coffee and beverages and food. Like the party the townsfolk had for them when they first got married. Cooper tried to maintain order of his town without the fussing and fighting a drinking saloon would cause. Every man here knew if they wanted to drink, they'd have to go somewhere else or stay at home.

He held out a chair and sat in the one across the table from her. She stared into his troubled eyes. She wanted to reach out and touch his hand, to take away some of the cause of his distress. Instead, Marie clasped her hands together on her lap. "Will you tell me now?"

"Is that you Doc Owen?" A voice, loud and authoritative, interrupted.

Owen turned toward the voice. "It is us."

A plump older woman with pure white hair pulled back in a bun came through a pair of saloon doors that led to the kitchen area. She was balancing a huge tray in both hands. She wore a stained apron over a dark blue dress with long sleeves and a collar that touched her double chin. "Good evening, Doc Owen. Marie. Supper is hot and ready to eat."

"Thank you, Millie," Owen told her.

As she was serving the plates, an old man came out from the same door holding a violin and sweet music slowly filled up the room. He stood a ways back, so as not to disturb the couple. Marie forgot for a moment how upset Owen was as she listened to the music.

When he finished, she clapped and gave Owen a huge smile. "Thank you. That was lovely."

"Let's dig into our food and we'll talk when we're finished."

"I'm still nervous about what you will tell me, Owen. It doesn't appear you are happy about things as they stand."

"Shhh," he told her, laying a hand over hers. "Let's enjoy this right now."

The man with the violin played a few more soft tunes until he backed out of the room while they ate. Marie always enjoyed being with Owen. He had so much to tell her about the people of this town. Every day he'd tell her about one of his patients, making her laugh, sometimes even shocking her at the stories as well.

Tonight, she was worried. There was so much more he wanted to tell her and yet he was making her wait. She put her fork down. Her plate was half-empty but she couldn't eat another bite until he confessed. "Owen. I'm not going to sit here and pretend nothing is wrong while you are keeping your troubles bottled up inside. It's time to spill the beans."

His whole body relaxed as he slumped back against the back of the chair. He took a cloth napkin and wiped his mouth. "You're right. I apologize, my dear. Let's get on with this."

When he didn't say anything else for a moment, she reached out and took his hand. "What are you finding so hard to tell me about?" She didn't realize how hard she was clenching her jaw until it began to hurt her mouth. Easing up, she looked into his eyes to see a tortured look in them.

She waited.

It was almost as if he was afraid to tell her. Didn't he want to be married to her any longer? Was he going to send her back to that horrible step-mother of hers? There was no way she'd ever return to that house again. Not by her own accord. Maybe it was good she had money stashed away after all.

Squaring her shoulders, she waited for him to speak.

"Marie, I have to tell you about my past."

She watched him carefully as he took in a deep breath. "Go on."

"A few years ago, while living in Kansas, someone came into my office at night while I was there and tried to rob me. He was a desperate man and knew I had opium among other tinctures and medicines in the apothecary there. He pulled a gun on me and fired the weapon when I caught him in the cabinet."

Marie's eyes widened. "I'm so sorry. You poor man!" She held onto his hand a bit tighter. It must've been terrifying!

Owen shook his head. "It was worse for the man. I always kept a gun in my desk. I grabbed it and shot without thinking. The man died that night by my hand."

Marie wasn't quite sure why it upset him so. "You did the right thing, Owen. He shot at you and perhaps he'd have killed you if he'd been a better shot. Then, we'd never be here in Cooper's Ridge together."

He lowered his head, letting out another huge sigh. Owen ran a hand over his hair. "He had a brother who is meaner than a rattlesnake's bite. He had gotten drunk earlier and was spending the night in jail. When he found out what happened, he hollered out of the jail window how I'd pay for killing his brother."

"He was in jail. What happened when he got out?"

Owen shook his head. "The sheriff found out he was a wanted man and they sent him to a prison a few states away. Luckily, it was one of the prisons where our pastor had ministered to at one time. He just got word Vic Townsly escaped a week ago. Word is he is coming this way to find me for killing his brother."

Marie had to admit she was frightened at the thought of a mean-hearted outlaw trying to bring harm to her husband. "I'm in shock, Owen. What do we do?"

"*We* don't do anything. He's going to come here, that we do know. A man like Vic won't stop until he finds me."

"Then, let's leave here. Today. We can go far away." She had to admit picking up and moving away saddened her heart. She was beginning to believe Cooper's Ridge was the home she always craved since her mother died. But her husband was in danger and he needed to be protected.

"I'm not going to run, Marie. Cooper has assured me he'd back me up. I'm not a fighter, I'm a doctor. What I won't do, however, is turn my back on a man who wants me dead. I'll have to face him."

The thought scared the daylights out of her. She put a hand on her bosom and whispered. "Owen, you can't possibly face such a dangerous man!"

"I won't be alone. Cooper Murphy has my back, along with many others from this town. If I have to face this outlaw, it will be better if I'm here with people who have my back."

"I'll also have your back. I don't know how to shoot a gun, but you do have time to teach me, don't you? We have to keep David out of this somehow. I don't want him to be scared."

"Not if I can help it, he won't be."

"I have to say I'm scared to death that something terrible will happen to you, Owen. I have grown to love you." If he didn't know that by now, she'd have to show him by standing by him through this.

Owen's face softened. He lifted a hand and brushed it across her cheek. "I have to put this in my past, Marie. So we can be free to love each other the way you deserve to be loved."

"What are you saying, Owen?" His words scared her.

"I'm saying, I want you and David to leave here. At least until this is over. If you don't go, I'll file for an annulment."

"What?"

She stood and shook a finger at him. "Owen, that is the stupidest thing I ever heard. What wife runs away when her husband is in trouble? This is my home too and I'm not leaving."

"Then I'll get a room at the boarding house until you do."

"That's brilliant! You're worried about putting me and David in danger yet you'd leave us in our home without a man here to protect us?"

Owen's eyes widened. "You're right. I'm afraid I'm not thinking straight."

"Darn right, you're not! Owen, I love you. Did you hear what I said? Because you haven't told me that you love me!"

He stood and looked into her eyes. "I've also grown to love you, Marie. Any man in his right mind would take all precautions to keep their family safe. I'm not going to the boarding house. I can't send you and David there in case the outlaws show up and try to board there. God knows someone in this town will open their mouth and tell them I'm married."

"Good, because I don't plan on going anywhere. I told you that."

"We have a few days, a week maybe before they figure out where Cooper's Ridge is. I'll think of something. Know this, Marie. You will not be here when they show up! That's my final word."

She was so tired of people bossing her around and telling her what to do! "Who do you think you are?"

He raised a brow. "I'm your husband. The man who has the final say!"

She opened her mouth to speak, then stomped her kid boot and picked up her skirts that made a whooshing noise throughout the quiet saloon. "In that case, I'll remove myself from your presence. I do not want to discuss this anymore tonight." Marie took off out the door faster than a woman should go in boots with a heel. Especially over a wobbly wooden porch.

She almost slipped and if Owen hadn't followed her outside and grabbed her in time, she'd have made a laughing stock of herself. He pulled her flush against his chest and stared into her eyes. "You are one feisty woman. Perhaps it's time to make you understand that you are my wife and you'll do as I say."

She rolled her eyes. Then, Marie smiled. "Owen, you may be my husband and I may have to listen to you according to the law, but I won't be tamed, if that's what you think."

He laughed.

She growled at him like a mountain lion ready to attack.

He leaned in and kissed her on the mouth.

She almost pushed away and then smashed her lips against his. Marie wrapped her arms around his neck and gave him a kiss worth waiting for.

She pushed away, gave him a long, cold stare and narrowed her eyes. "You just remember, Owen Gordon, you may try to boss me around, but it won't work. I'm going home!"

As she turned to go up the few steps to their porch, he caught up to her, picked her up off the ground and carried her over the threshold, then the door slammed behind with a huge bang.

Chapter 12

Marie hadn't realized it was so late. She jumped up out of bed and quickly washed up and got dressed, wondering if Owen was downstairs since his side of the bed was empty. She smiled remembering their first real night together.

They were now truly husband and wife. She gazed at herself in the mirror, brushed her hair and pinched her cheeks. He had told her at the saloon he'd file for an annulment if she didn't leave. It was too late for that.

There was still time to convince Owen not to face Vic Townsly. He should let the men who know how to go after outlaws deal with his kind. After all, shouldn't there be a sheriff or lawman here to handle such problems?

Marie decided she wanted to look different this morning. She braided her hair loosely and pulled a yellow ribbon from her bag, then proceeded to wind it around her braid, letting the ends hang down her back. She'd save the skirt and blouse Ophelia bought for her for special occasions only. For today, she wore a pale yellow skirt and matching blouse she bought ready made at the dress shop down the street when she first arrived. She pushed her feet into her favorite slippers and slowly made her way downstairs.

An adorable little black and tan face with a red tongue hanging out looked up at her from the bottom step, its tail wagging so fast she thought it may just fly off into the air. He let out some high-pitched barks so she picked him up and made her way to the kitchen. There was a cup of coffee sitting on the table along with a small flower in another cup. The flower actually was a weed from the back yard, but the thought made Marie smile regardless.

She sat down and took a sip of the lukewarm coffee, not caring that it was no longer hot. This was the first time Owen had prepared her coffee. She was usually up before him most mornings so this meant a lot to her. She was going to sit and enjoy every sip of it until she had to get up to start her chores.

Marie was startled when someone began pounding on the front door. The pup jumped down from her lap and flew across the floor as he raced to see who was there. His little feet and paws slid all over the place until they froze to the floor as he barked at whoever was outside.

They rapped again, a little louder. What if it was the outlaw coming to find Owen? She shook her head, realizing any outlaw coming into town would have to ride past the church where Pastor Murphy kept a careful watch. He'd most likely never get close enough to the doctor's office before he was stopped.

Even so, she was cautious when opening the door. Since it was Saturday and there were no doctor hours for today, the front door was always kept locked. Now, she turned the door handle and opened up far enough to see who was there.

"Hello, Mrs. Gordon. You have a telegram!"

She came face to face with Arthur Abbot from the telegraph office. "Good morning, sir. The telegram is for me?"

"Yes, ma'am. Here you go."

She took the paper he handed to her and was about to close the door when she noticed he stood staring. Then he began to shake his leg, causing the little dog to yelp and run behind Marie's skirts. It was almost funny but Arthur looked horrified.

"Don't worry, Arthur. We have a puppy now."

"Scared the daylights out of me. I'll be going now." He walked backwards down the street, then turned and walked as fast as humanly possible. Arthur was cussing up a storm. She heard him grumble to himself about animals in the house. She giggled. Nothing was going to ruin her wonderful mood this morning.

"Who is here?" Owen came out of his office holding a pistol in his hand. A bit late. What was he doing in there that he hadn't heard the noise at the door?

"It was a telegram. For me. Please put that away, Owen. You told me we'd have a week until this outlaw shows up."

"I assumed a week. That doesn't mean he can't find his way here sooner. Next time wait for me before you open the door."

"He was knocking on the door for some time before I opened it. I'm surprised you didn't hear. What will you do on Monday morning when patients are expected? We can't keep the door locked during work hours."

"I'll worry about it on Monday. Aren't you going to read your telegram?"

She did. When she read the words written, her heart stopped then began to pump so hard she thought she was going to have to sit down. "Oh no!"

"What is it, Marie? What has you so upset?"

She handed the paper to him. "I never thought I'd see that witch again! This is horrible!"

He looked surprised at her words but he had no idea how conniving and mean her step-mother was. She didn't want her home turned upside down. She closed her eyes as he read it aloud. *"Your stepmother and I will be arriving any day. We will be needing a place to stay. Please have something ready. Your Father."* Stop.

Owen stared at her.

"Please. Don't say anything. I know I should be happy my father is coming to visit. Why he's coming, I don't understand.

He sent me away without a care. He couldn't afford to keep me or Dora, so I don't understand why he'd travel across the country to visit? Where did he get the money to travel? Dear Lord, he is visiting, isn't he? Let me see that telegram!"

She read it twice before realizing his words were quite vague. "It doesn't make any sense."

"I'm sure there is a reasonable explanation. If you'll excuse me I'll go to the boarding house now and secure a room for when they arrive. It appears to me the idea of hosting your step-mother will be too taxing for you."

He took a hat from the hook beside the door and gave her a sweet peck on the cheek. "We can't have you too upset now, can we? Especially if we plan to have children."

She swiped at him but missed. "Owen. Behave that tongue of yours," she warned.

He grinned and leaned in for another kiss. "Make sure to lock the door behind me."

"I will. Would you mind stopping by the neighbor's and bring David home? I'm anxious for him to meet this little pup. Maybe he'll follow David around instead of me."

The puppy jumped up onto Marie's skirts. She leaned over and patted him on the head, causing him to sit. "There! Look at what you did. Good boy."

When Owen left, she went back to the kitchen to make another cup of coffee. The moment she had it done, there was another knock on the door. It usually wasn't this busy on a Saturday. Marie barely had time to think let alone enjoy her coffee.

She remembered what Owen said about being cautious and leaned into the front window to peek through the glass. "Cynthia?" Quickly she opened the door and motioned for her friend to come inside. When she was in the foyer, Marie locked the door behind her.

"I don't usually stop by on a Saturday as you know. I really must speak to you."

"I have hot coffee."

Cynthia followed Marie to the kitchen. "Let me get the cups," she offered, helping Marie. They sat across from each other then poured cream and a spoonful of sugar in the black liquid. Marie watched her friend carefully.

"What's going on, Cynthia? You look upset."

Cynthia gazed around the room then down the hallway. "Is your husband here?" she whispered.

Marie shook her head. "He went to the boarding house to secure a room for my father who is arriving any day to visit."

"How lovely."

"Not as lovely as you think. What's on your mind?"

"I'm with child."

"How wonderful! When did you find out?"

"I'm pretty certain I am, but Tom doesn't know yet. I want to be sure."

"Did you stop in on a Saturday to have my husband examine you?"

"Yes. Discreetly of course. I don't want anyone to see me here as a patient."

Cynthia had told Marie how scared she was to have a baby since she didn't want to share her husband quite yet. She didn't have any advice for her friend since she wasn't in that kind of position. Marie was anxious to have a child and would shout it to the rooftops when it happens.

Owen came back ten minutes later and jiggled the door knob, then used his own key to get in. "David will be along shortly. His friends also want to see the dog."

Marie met him in the hallway, whispering softly. He nodded and went into his office. "Cynthia? He'll see you now."

While Cynthia was in the examining room, the door flung open and David and his two friends came running down the hallway. David was so excited but when he laid eyes on the little pup, they got so huge she thought he would pop an eye out. "Is that my dog?"

Marie smiled. "It's our family dog, David. That means you'll be responsible to help take care of him."

"How do I do that?" His words came out softly as he took a few steps closer. The pup was sleeping on her lap until he realized there were others in the room. His ears perked up and he sat up then began barking at the boys.

They all three laughed out loud. One of the boys was laughing so hard he bent over holding his gut.

"Can I hold him?" David stood right next to the little pup.

"Yes. Pick him up gently and let him get to know you," Marie told him.

When David picked up the puppy, a tongue licked him on the nose. He giggled while the other boys laughed. After they all got a turn holding him, David asked if they were allowed to take him outside in the yard to play.

"Only in the back yard where I can see you." They ran outside, the little pup right behind them. It's tail was wagging so hard again it made the boys laugh harder. The joy she saw in David's face was all the reward she ever wanted. He seemed truly happy.

Watching the boys play with the pup through the kitchen window, it occurred to Marie that maybe Owen was right. Although she wanted to stay and protect her husband, David deserved a family. He didn't need trouble or to have anyone torn from him again. They had to find a way to get through this together.

But first, they had to deal with her father and step-mother. What would happen if the outlaw and her father showed up at the same time? Things were getting quite difficult and she wasn't sure which way to go. How were they going to deal with an outlaw and her step-mother at the same time?

To be honest, she wasn't sure which one was the worst of the two!

Chapter 13

David was still outside with his friends playing with the puppy when Owen came out from his office. Cynthia had gone home to tell Tom the news after speaking with the doctor about her situation. She must've felt more confident since then, as she decided it was better to be honest and tell her husband the truth. Marie thought it was a good decision.

When her husband came into the kitchen, she was standing by the window watching the boys play. He wrapped his arms around her waist and kissed her gently on the cheek.

She turned in his arms. "Thank you."

He looked confused. "For what?"

"For helping Cynthia. She didn't want to tell Tom she was with child yet. I believe you changed her mind."

He grinned. "It's because I'm a pretty good doctor if I must say so."

"You're the best doctor this town ever had."

Owen laughed. "I'm the only doctor this town ever had. This town isn't that old." He looked out the window when he heard someone yell. Marie felt his body go rigid.

"It's just the boys having fun," she told him.

"Is that why you're standing here watching them?"

She nodded. "I guess the outlaw that wants to hurt you has me a bit shook up. Especially since David has friends and is constantly on the go. I'm not sure how to keep him safe without explaining the truth to him."

"Marie, it's why I'd rather you not be here. If he finds out who you are or who David is, he may try to use either one of you against me."

She closed her eyes, not wanting to leave here. Yet, when she opened her eyes and saw David and how happy he was now, the thought of uprooting him tore at her heart. Then, the thought of an outlaw hurting him to get at Owen gave her even more terror inside. "Maybe we should send David somewhere safe."

"I wish to send you both somewhere safe. On my way back from the boarding house, I ran into Cooper and his wife, Catherine. She suggested you and the boy stay at Nora White's ranch until the outlaw business is taken care of. She has assured me it is far enough away from Cooper's Ridge that you'll be safe."

"How far away?"

"A few miles down the road. You'll be safe there and David will have enough to keep him busy. He can take the pup. There are cows and horses and he can stay busy helping the ranch hands and cowboys. It will be good for him."

"I don't want to leave you alone to deal with this bad man."

He hugged her a little tighter. "I've realized how much you mean to me. And the boy. As a man, please understand it is my duty to make sure you and my son are safe. It doesn't matter what happens to me. I'm resigned to protect you."

"It matters to me. I'm starting to understand what you're telling me, Owen. I love David as if he were my own."

"I feel the same way about the boy and I love you, Marie. We have some time though. Cooper got word this morning that Townsly is still in Kansas."

Marie was so confused. "How in the world can Pastor Murphy know this?"

"He has a lot of friends and he used to work on the side of the law. He knows a lot of people. He's been having Townsly tracked. Telegrams were the best thing invented, don't you think?"

She nodded.

He ran a hand down her cheek. "Don't worry. We'll have plenty of time to get you to safety. By the time he gets to Wichita Falls or Mill Ridge, both sheriffs' know to send word. He'll most likely come that way since he makes it a point to stir up trouble in every town he rides through, then slips out of town before he is caught. Around here, things are a bit different. Sheriff Montgomery from Wichita Falls plans to send a telegram when the outlaw gets to his town. So don't worry too much."

"Are you certain?"

"I've finally realized this town is my home and the people here and in the area are looking out for all of us. They wouldn't steer us wrong, Marie. Besides, Townsly may do something stupid like rob a train or bank before he gets here. If he does, he's back in jail or dead. I promise you everything will be all right."

She hugged him, glad they had more time together. "If I have to go to this ranch you suggested, I'll worry every single moment until that man is caught."

They held each other for a moment until continuous banging on the front door had Marie jumping back. Owen stiffened again and gave Marie a stern look. "Stay here and watch the children. I'll answer the door."

She watched, angry that the outlaw was causing them to be fearful in their own home. After peeking out the window to make sure David was safe, she moved to the hallway to see who was at the door. Owen held a pistol in his left hand when he opened the door, then tucked it in his waist behind him. Marie stretched her neck to see who was outside.

She recognized the face. Another telegram? Just then, the boys came inside, laughing and pointing at the puppy as he scrambled

THE RUNAWAY

across the kitchen floor. They all laughed hilariously when the pup ran into the wall and flopped on his bottom, then starting yawning.

"Boys, I believe he's tired. How about letting the pup get some rest? David, say good-bye to your friends."

The three of them began to complain until Owen walked down the hall and stood in the kitchen. Marie watched in amusement as they all said goodbye and the two other boys left, slamming the front door behind them.

"May I take Goliath into the parlor?"

Owen nodded. "Goliath? That's a huge name for a little puppy."

"I think he's going to grow up big and strong. I'm already his friend so he doesn't have to grow into a big giant like the story says. He can be my friend because we love each other."

Owen and Marie looked at each other. She was anxious to hear what the telegram was about and smiled at David's ideas. If he wanted to call the pup Goliath that was fine by her. "Goliath is a great name, David."

The boy left carrying the pup in his arms. Goliath looked like he was utterly exhausted. Marie watched until they both disappeared. She turned to Owen. "What does the telegram say?"

"Can we go out onto the porch?"

Marie began to worry. She followed him outside, making sure to look up and down the street in case there was an unfamiliar face in town. There wasn't, but she was being cautious anyway. She noticed Owen did the same thing, which told her he didn't quite trust things to work out the way Pastor Murphy said it would. There was always a slim chance the outlaw would slip through town without anyone knowing.

"I see in your face you're being cautious."

"I see the same in yours."

"I know what you're thinking. That the outlaw may slip through without anyone seeing him and catch me unaware."

"I see your are thinking the exact same thing."

"You're right. It's hard to put trust into a town like this or Wichita Falls or Mill Ridge when no one has ever had your back before. I'm trying to trust them. I haven't been here that long to be able to. All I know is there are good men all around us. We have to try."

She stood alongside of him, wondering when the fear and worry would go away. All of her life she thought she was loved and then when her mother passed away and her father remarried, he had pushed her away and left a horrible step-mother to take over. The last few years had been so hard. She lost so much and yet standing here looking out at the dusty town before her, she never felt so loved and cherished.

She was so scared it would all be taken away. Just like her mother had been. This time it would be much worse.

*****

Owen stood beside his wife, watching her staring into the street and trembling slightly when a memory came to her. He knew she was worried and concerned for her son. She should be. Vic Townsly was no one to mess with. He felt the same way she did right now. It had been a few years since he felt the sense of home and family.

He was worried it would be taken away, one piece at a time. Or, with one shot. Like he took Charlie Townsly's life from him. Even though the man was a con-artist and outlaw, a life was sacred according to the Bible. Would God forgive him for what he did when it was Owen's turn to stand before Him someday?

Owen knew he was justified. But during times like this, the heavy weight of what he did was on his shoulders. He wanted to make things right, but it was too late. Charlie was dead and his brother was coming to avenge that death.

They say a man's days are numbered. Were his?

"Owen?"

He realized she'd been speaking and turned to her, taking her hand.

"What does the telegram say? Please tell me my father and step-mother changed their mind?"

"That would be too simple. I'm afraid this telegram is from the New York Juvenile Asylum. They are sending an agent for David's yearly check-in."

"Oh, dear! Yearly? He's only been with us for a few months. What are they thinking? This is not a good time! What happens if they come during this whole fiasco? Can they take David away from us?"

"They would be fools to do such a thing. Don't worry, it's not for another three weeks. By that time, Vic Townsly will be locked up and your parents will be long gone. Hopefully."

Marie let out a sigh. Owen saw her free hand was still clutched onto the railing, her knuckles white. He pulled her into his arms. "Let's take this one day at a time. We've both been through much worse."

"Do we tell David?"

Owen shook his head. "Not right now. Let him rest. We'll discuss it after supper tonight." His wife would have the rest of the day to calm herself. Owen knew it wouldn't do David any good to see his parents upset. The boy came a long way. He had friends now and a home he could call his own. But if he were threatened, and with his past as a runaway, Owen wasn't sure what to expect. They had to remain calm, cool and collected.

Marie smiled. She placed his face in between both her hands and pinched his cheeks. It made him chuckle. "You are a smart man. If David sees I'm upset, he'll get frightened. You're giving us time to calm ourselves."

"I'm giving *you* time to collect yourself, darling. Now go on and get some boots on. I want to take you and David on a buggy ride to visit the White Ranch."

The afternoon was filled with an hours drive to the ranch, and total chaos as David and his pup Goliath were swept off by a few of the ranch hands. He was so excited to see and touch so many horses and cattle up close.

Marie and Owen met the owners of the ranch, Nora and Rusty. He was an older red-haired fellow with a jolly smile and Nora was tall and regal and very self-assured. They invited Owen and Marie to have some lemonade on the porch while David was busy in the barn.

"Pastor Murphy explained your situation. I want you to know you'll be safe here," she told them, looking directly into Marie's eyes.

Marie squeezed Owen's hand. She was nervous to discuss their situation so openly. He gave her a reassuring smile. "It's okay, Marie. I've been told some wonderful stories about this ranch and how everyone here protected this place when evil came knocking. I feel good about leaving you and David here if it comes to that."

She was watching him closely as if looking for him to be telling her a fake story. He squeezed her hand again. She nodded and let out a sigh. Turning to Nora, they became quite involved in a deep conversation as Rusty told him stories of their recent cattle drive.

Everyone had supper outside where a few tables were set up. Afterwards, one of the ranch hands played a guitar while David and Goliath ran around in circles. Finally, Owen stood up. He reached out a hand to Rusty. "Thank you for having us. I feel better now that we've met. Thank you for everything."

Marie stood too. She looked surprised when Nora pulled her into a hug and whispered something in her ear. It brought a huge smile to Marie's face.

They had to practically pull David away and he looked so upset when he had to leave. It was the perfect time to explain a few things. Owen suggested he sit in the middle between them. When David was comfortable with Goliath on his lap, the boy looked up and asked if they were going to go back there again.

Owen loved the boy's timing. "Of course. As a matter of fact, I may have something important to do in the near future and if you'd like to stay at the White Ranch while I'm busy, you and Marie can sleep over at the ranch. How would you like that?"

His eyes got huge. "What about Goliath? Can he come too?"

Marie reassured him that the pup goes too.

"Will it be tomorrow?"

"No, son. I'll tell you when you have to, er, can go to visit for a short period of time. We'll pack an overnight bag and you and Marie can spend all the time you want there."

"Are you going to go too when you're done doing important things?" He looked somewhat worried, which made Owen's throat constrict.

"Of course I'll come to the ranch the moment I'm done."

"Okay."

Marie looked as if she were going to laugh out loud at the way David accepted everything. It had been a good idea to take him for a visit first. Now he had to tell the boy about the other upcoming visitor. Hopefully the news wouldn't matter too much.

"There's another visitor coming to see us soon, David."

"Do you mean Marie's father? I heard you talk about him. My friend says that he is my grandfather."

Owen nodded. "That's right, David. But, your grandfather will be here in a few days, but in a few weeks an agent from New York is stopping in to check and make sure we are taking good care of you."

Owen tried to keep it simple. Except, he saw the look of horror on David's face. He pulled the puppy closer to his chest and Owen swore there were tears in his eyes. "You mean from the home? Why do they have to come here? I don't want them to come."

Marie gathered him in her arms. "They always make a visit once you are settled in to make sure you are taken care of, David."

"Can't we just send them a letter? My teacher can write really good."

Owen stopped the buggy. David wasn't taking this too well. "David, listen to me. Look at me."

When his big brown eyes stared into Owen's it made his heart wretch. "I promise you with all my heart that no one, and I mean *no one* will ever take you back to that place. And if they try, I'll hide you out at the ranch we were just at and those cowboys there will never let you come to harm, okay?"

He shook his head. "Will you punch the agent if he tries."

Marie's eyes got wide. "Why would you say that, David?"

He smiled then. "Because the cowboys at the ranch said they are cow punchers and if they can punch a cow, then why can't we punch an agent?"

"Why don't we take David for a special treat tonight? The church is having a dessert social. Would you like to go, David?"

The special request caught his attention. Away from the cow punch theory to Owen's relief. "Yes. Can Goliath come too?"

"Of course. As long as he behaves."

Marie and Owen stared at each other.

It was going to be a long night trying to explain to David about a cow punch.

Chapter 14

"Marie? What are you doing here?" She was shocked to see them here mid-morning.

"You sent me here, don't you remember?" Marie would be polite for her father's sake, but she wasn't going to put up with any shenanigans in her own home. Especially from the woman standing at her front door.

"Hello. Are you my grandfather and grandmother?" David's words had Marie cringing. She gave her son a weak smile.

"Yes. This is your grandfather and Constance." There was no way that woman would claim to be David's grandmother, not as long as Marie was alive.

She looked at her father and was quite taken back by his thin frame. He wore one of the same suits he always wore to the bank every day. Gray with a white shirt and black tie. Except the suit he had on was wrinkled as if he hadn't changed clothes in a very long time. It hung off his shoulders and the pants were quite baggy. She almost felt sorry for him. Some type of bad luck had struck the man who raised her.

"Won't you please come in," she offered, opening the door wide enough to allow them both entrance.

"Want to see Goliath?" David's huge smile turned into a frown when Constance gave him a long hard stare.

"Young man, where are your manners? You should only speak when spoken to." She brushed past Marie and David, then waltzed into the parlor as if she owned the house.

Marie looked at her father, ready to instruct him to do something about her, but when she saw his face she kept quiet. He was already a broken man. It wasn't the father that had raised her standing before her. What had Constance done to him in such a short period of time?

Marie was angry. Not only had the terrible woman sent her away from the only home she knew, Constance had caused her father terrible distress. Perhaps it was time to find out what was going on. Where in the world was Owen? He went to meet them at the boarding house twenty minutes ago.

"Did my husband meet you at the boarding house?"

Constance gave her an alarming look. "Your husband? Who in the world would marry you?" She laughed as if joking, but Marie knew she meant every word.

David squirmed while trying to hold onto the pup. She ignored Constance and looked at David. "I would like you to take Goliath for a nap. Would you mind taking him to your room?"

His little eyes lit up. "You never let me take him upstairs. Can I? Really?"

"Of course. Just for today."

It didn't take long for David to scramble off the settee and run up the steps. At least with the boy in his room, she didn't have to worry about Constance saying anything awful around him. He had been through enough bad treatment and Marie wasn't going to allow Constance near him.

How was she going to get this woman out of her house? Just as she was about to ask if they were thirsty, Owen came in the door struggling with some luggage.

"There's my luggage. Thank you, Doctor. Now that there is an adult here, will you point me in the direction of your wife? I'd like to see my daughter."

Owen set the three pieces of luggage beside the front door. He swiped at his hands and stuck them in his pocket then faced Constance. "My wife is standing right beside you."

"What? No, that's not your wife. It's Marie, for heaven's sake!"

"Yes, Marie is my wife."

Owen didn't look too happy. What was happening and why was luggage at her front door? A dread filled her up like nobody's business. She stared at her husband.

He gave her the kind of look that said it all. "I'm so sorry, Marie. We'll have to put your parents up here for a few days until the boarding house empties out. It seems the proprietress booked all the rooms and forgot about your family coming today. It won't be long, just a day or two."

Marie tried not to show any emotion. How was she going to keep her sanity with Constance in the house? She turned to her father. "I can offer you David's room. He'll have to move in with us while you're here."

Her father nodded. "Anything will do, Marie. Thank you for putting us up."

"This is so confusing." Constance demanded their attention. "Where is Dora?"

"Dora is in Kansas married to a cattle rancher."

"What?" Constance sat down on the settee. "What is she doing there? She was supposed to be here!"

Marie was about to enjoy her next words. "Your daughter did not go through with her promise to marry Owen. She met a rich man on the train and decided she wanted him instead. She would've left me stranded if I hadn't demanded she hand over the money my father left for me."

Her father frowned. "Why didn't you have the money, Marie? I gave it to you."

She gave Constance an accusing look. "Your wife grabbed it from my hand before I was able to walk out the door and gave it all to Dora. She didn't think I deserved a dime. I believe those were her words. She saw Ophelia give me a gift and said that was all I deserved."

Her father hung his head. "I'm sorry, Marie."

"Don't be sorry! Dora deserved the money more."

"That's enough, Constance."

Marie was surprised when he stood up to her. Her father already had more trouble than he deserved, so Marie spoke up. "I'm sure the two of you are hungry. I'll make something for you to eat and then get my son's room ready."

"Your son? That little boy with the mutt is your son?" Constance looked appalled.

"Yes, he most certainly is." She looked at her father. "I'll explain all about David when I'm done." When Marie left the room it was with her head held high. Constance hissed at her when she walked by. Instead of noticing, Marie ignored her. She wasn't about to let that old cranky woman ruin this visit from her father.

Besides, Marie was reeling in the satisfaction that her rose bush was sitting right outside of her kitchen window slowly growing into the beautiful bush it once was when her mother cared for it.

As she put worked in the kitchen, Marie wondered if this was just a visit. The thought they were coming here to live with Dora had occurred to her. She knew things were not going well at the bank and that's why she was sent with Dora in the first place. Had things gotten worse?

When Owen came into the kitchen while she was setting the table, she pulled him aside. "Please tell me why they have no place to go?"

"I'm sorry, Marie. I didn't want to stand on the street all day. Constance was starting to make a scene at the boarding house. When I came along, I tried to restore order and invited them to share David's room. David can share our room for now. I won't have him sleeping in the same room with that witch."

Marie started laughing.

Owen cracked a smile. "I probably went too far, didn't I?"

"Not at all. You reminded me how Ophelia used to call her a witch."

"I wanted to get you to smile, otherwise I'm afraid you may lose your temper. I see the anger you have in your eyes for that woman. We'll feed her and find a solution to keep the two of you at a distance."

"I'm terrified that something happened and they'll want to stay. Not that I don't love my father, I do. We have to get them out of here. What if the outlaw shows up?"

"Don't worry yourself. Let me do the worrying. Promise?"

She nodded, then gave him a peck on the cheek. "I promise for now. Would you call them out here, please?"

Marie had sliced some fresh bread and warmed up some leftover soup from the night before that was simmering on the stove for their mid-day meal. She added two extra place settings, then pushed a long bench that had been against the wall to the one side of the table.

Owen seated their guests while Marie went to David's room to explain what was happening. He didn't seem too worried and told her since it was his grandfather, he didn't mind giving up his room. She tousled his hair. "You are a good boy, David. Don't ever let anyone tell you that you're not."

"I won't. I wonder if Goliath can sleep with me, too. He doesn't like that lady."

Marie wanted to tell him that no one liked that lady, but knew it wasn't proper to say so. She ground her teeth together instead. "Are you hungry? There's soup and fresh bread waiting for us."

David picked up his pup and they went down to the kitchen while Marie tidied up his room. She took an extra blanket from their bedroom and a pillow from her bed and placed it on David's bed. It wasn't a huge bed, but would have to do. There was nowhere else for her father to go. This town wasn't that big and only had the boarding house for visitors.

When she heard a yelp, Marie hurried down the steps, then almost ran down the hall. She heard Owen scold David. "Please take Goliath outside."

"By his self? But, he didn't do anything!"

"David." The warning was clear in Owen's voice. David scooted his chair back and put the puppy outside, then slumped in his seat when he came back to the table.

Marie sat beside her husband, then offered a prayer. Owen served the soup and they ate silently. She saw David was squirming in his seat, anxious to be with his dog. She didn't blame him for being upset. They never had to keep the pup outside without David. What if Goliath ran off? She wasn't sure what had happened but there was no doubt in her mind it had something to do with Constance.

That woman always had evil intent in her eyes.

"Owen, I didn't know you had a son. It wasn't in any of the letters you had sent to Dora." She glanced at Marie to let her know Owen had originally desired Dora as his mail-order bride.

"David was a gift from God to this family. He lived in New York City before coming here on the orphan train. Marie met him on the train. Now we are one happy family. Isn't that right, Marie?"

"We certainly are." She stared right back at Constance, feeling like a petulant child. It couldn't be helped. That woman had been her nightmare for two long years. It didn't hurt to dish a little back to her now.

Except she saw the shame in her father's eyes and regretted making an ordeal of things. Didn't God say to forgive and forget? Seven times seventy-times-seven or something of that order? Now she was ashamed of her behavior. It was time to let by-gones be by-gones. *Lord, give me the strength to do your will, not mine. But if she tries to harm or shame David, I'll personally throw her out onto the street without flinching.*

Then she asked the Lord to forgive her for putting conditions on her prayer. She was so mixed up. Constance was a nuisance to her and always would be. The woman tore her family apart. It was so odd that Dora hadn't written home. Why hadn't she?

"I assume you haven't heard from Dora since you thought she was here happily married to the doctor?"

Her father shook his head. "We haven't. Not one word. When the bank closed, we decided to sell the house before it was taken and follow Dora here. Constance wanted to check up on her."

"Father, the bank closed? I'm so sorry to hear that. Wasn't there any other openings in New York?" It was so odd they left a prosperous city so quickly.

"I'm afraid a much larger bank was built in our area and gave the customers discounts and deals my small bank was unable to compete with. Like I said, it was no longer feasible to stay in banking. I cashed out some of my investments after the house was sold and paid for. We have some traveling money, but we thought it might be more affordable to live here. Constance misses her daughter."

Owen added to the conversation. "Since Dora is not here, perhaps Marie knows the man she married and their location."

Constance gave Marie a promising look. "Do you remember the fellow, dear?"

The lemonade going down her throat caused a coughing fit Marie almost choked on. Constance had called her many names but none of them were ever *dear*. But she'd do or say anything to get rid of the woman. "Yes, I do remember."

Then Marie got quiet and kept drinking her lemonade.

Owen chuckled.

Her father smiled. He tried not to but it appeared that he couldn't help himself. She looked into his eyes and saw a slight sparkle that wasn't there before. Perhaps he liked the idea of someone having the upper hand over his wife.

Marie stood. "I'll tell you exactly where Dora is after you apologize to my son."

Constance blinked twice before giving Marie a dark look. "Why should I apologize to the boy. He had that awful dog in this house. The dog bit me."

"I don't believe the dog bit you, Constance. Either you apologize or Dora's whereabouts stay a mystery."

She didn't dare turn her head to see what Owen or her father were doing.

"Very well. If it gets me closer to Dora, I'll apologize. When I'm good and ready," she added.

Marie shook a finger at her. "Right now." She turned to David. "Please stand, David. Constance has something she wants to say to you."

He stood, perplexed and his eyes kept moving towards the yard outside where the pup was scratching at the back door.

Marie never believed for one moment Goliath bit that woman. For one, she was so sour, not even a puppy would try to bite her!

The thought made Marie laugh and she tried to hold her composure as she waited for Constance to speak.

"I'm sorry, boy. I apologize for whatever I did to your animal."

"His name is David. Please address him as such."

Constance glared. Her shoulders went up and she sighed. "David, I'm very sorry I got upset with your dog. There, will that suit?"

"Thank you. The dog is a part of our family and will not be put outside while we eat, sleep or have visitors. Do I make myself clear?"

Constance nodded.

"David, you may go get Goliath."

"Okay, mommy." David ran to the back door, let in Goliath and they both ran down the hallway out of sight.

His words hit her like a tornado taking a roof off a house. She glanced at Owen, who stood up at David's words. When Marie's lower lip began to quiver, he pulled her into his arms and held her there.

"Goodness gracious, what is the big ordeal? I've got a headache. I'm going to my room. Will we be staying in the room on the left or right of the stairs?"

When no one answered, Constance made loud noises with her heels across the kitchen floor and down the hall but no one was concerned with her departure. Marie was too overwhelmed to pay any attention. "He just called me mommy," she whispered.

"It's about time," Owen told her. "You deserve this moment."

Chapter 15

Marie turned to her father. "Forgive me. My son finally called me mommy. I've been waiting for those words for a long time."

Her father nodded. "I'm happy if it makes you happy, Marie. I want to apologize for the way Constance behaves. She hasn't been a good step-mother to you. I can see that now. Will you ever forgive me for what I've done to you?"

"Oh, Father!" She slipped from Owen's arms and embraced her father, something she didn't do very often. "I do forgive you."

He held her for so long she thought he would never let go. "I miss your mother. When she passed on to heaven's gate, I'm afraid I worried about taking care of you and married the first woman I met. I thought having Dora in the house would bring you some joy. Except it worked the opposite. I see that now. Before, I was too busy trying to keep up with the cost of having a new wife and another daughter."

Owen excused himself to open his practice which didn't open for another hour, but Marie knew he was trying to give them privacy. She mouthed thank you to him as he turned away.

She took both her father's hands. "What ever happened is in the past, Father. The truth is, it led me here. I'm so fortunate that Dora left Owen high and dry. Look what I have!"

"You seem to be doing quite well for yourself. Your mother would be proud."

"What about you, Father? Are you proud of me?"

He nodded. "Yes."

"Then that's what matters the most."

A hard knock on the front door caught Marie's attention. "It's probably my friend Cynthia coming to visit," she told her father.

THE RUNAWAY

"She visits a few times a week. Wait until you meet her." She hurried to the front door, surprised Cynthia didn't just walk in after knocking a few times. If it wasn't her, then whoever was out there was persistent. She peeked out the window just to be on the safe side and saw a strange women standing there.

When she opened the door a lovely strange woman stood on the porch. She wore a dark jacket over an immaculate white blouse and a long skirt that matched her jacket. Her hair was pulled back hard into a chignon while her eyes were so huge Marie felt as if they were staring right into her soul. The woman's shoulders were stiff and her chin was in the air. She was beautiful except for the sour look on her face.

Oh, dear! Who in the world was this? "Are you here to see the doctor?" Marie asked pleasantly.

"No, ma'am. I'm here to visit the orphan boy we sent to the Gordon family."

"You must be inquiring about David?"

"If that is his name, then, yes. There is only *boy* written on my paperwork."

"He is here playing in his room at the moment. Please, do come in." Marie's heart sank. She wasn't expecting the agent to show up now. Not when Constance was in the house.

The agent entered the house, her eyes moving around like a mouse looking for a piece of cheese. She held a clipboard in her hand along with a pencil between her fingers.

"We weren't expecting you for another few weeks."

"Exactly." She gave Marie a smile and continued looking around. "We like to have an element of surprise. It assures the New York Juvenile Asylum the children are in the right hands."

Marie's father walked down the hallway. "Can I help?"

She shook her head. "Would you mind asking Owen to come to the kitchen." She knew her voice was quite stiff at the moment. This woman scared her. Owen had told her the agents make one visit per year to make sure the children are being taken care of. It had only been a few months. Why was she here already?

"I sure will. Anything to help." He knocked on Owen's office door while Marie had the agent follow her to the parlor. "Would you like a cup of coffee or tea while I get David?"

"No thank you. I'd like to get on with this visit."

"Fine. If you'll excuse me, I'll fetch my son. You are welcome to have a seat if you like."

"Thank you."

Marie hurried upstairs to their room where David and Goliath were playing quietly on the floor. Her son was throwing one of her ballerina slippers across the floor while the pup went after it. David was giggling quietly, which was unusual. She normally heard him laughing at the dog a mile away.

She got down to his eye level. "David. Is everything all right?" It was hard not to mention her slippers were not dog toys. She'd talk to him about that later.

He shrugged. "That mean lady told me to be quiet. She wants to sleep."

"She needs her rest. Maybe she'll be in a better frame of mind if she gets some rest."

"I don't like her."

"It's best not to let her know that. If you give a smile no matter what, it will be returned to you in some other way."

He frowned. "You mean if I smile at everyone, I'll get things? Like more puppies or toys like the wooden trains at the store?"

That was not what she meant. "I'll try to explain these things later when we don't have company, David. Meanwhile, we have a visitor and I want you to be on your best behavior. Can you do that for me?"

He nodded, his eyes going huge. "Is someone coming to take me away?"

"David? What did Owen tell you about that? Do you remember?"

"Kind of. He said he wouldn't let no one take me back to the city."

She gave him a smile. "That's exactly right. We have a good home and Owen has a decent job. There is no reason anyone would take you away. Be nice and smile at the agent from the orphanage. She's in our parlor, okay?"

He held Goliath. "I want to take Goliath to show her I'm responsible."

"Please keep him under control."

"I will. I promise."

Marie brushed his hair and tidied his shirt, tucking it in neatly. She had him wash his hands and face in the bowl on her dresser where she kept a pitcher of fresh water for that purpose. Which reminder her she needed to freshen the pitcher for her guest.

Marie hoped and prayed Constance stayed in David's room but before they were halfway down the stairs, she heard the door open and close. "Is that boy making noise? Whose running up and down the stairway?"

"Go on downstairs, David. I'll be right there."

David skipped down the rest of the way, confident now that she told him no one was going to take him away.

She turned. "Constance? Please keep your voice down. An agent from the orphanage is here to visit with David. She'll most likely want to see his room."

"There's no getting any rest here, is there?" She stomped down the steps, her heels clicking on the wooden steps loud enough to wake the dead in the cemetery at the end of town. Unfortunately, she stood alongside of Marie in the parlor.

David was kneeling at the woman's feet while Goliath sat on his hind legs allowing her to pet him. She didn't smile, but looked up when the two ladies entered. Owen came in from the hallway and introduced himself.

The agent's face lit up when she saw Owen. Marie stood and watched the two converse. He offered to show her the house. Their guest didn't hesitate but followed him from room to room. Marie was not going to be left behind. Constance followed Marie, listening to the conversation between Owen and the agent.

Owen looked down at her repeating the name she had given him upon shaking his hand. Something she hadn't done with Marie. "Miss Clayton. It's a pleasure to have you here. Wait until you see how well David has done in school."

"Why isn't David in school? And, please, it's Winifred Clayton. You may call me Winnie if you'd like."

"Thank you, Winnie. I'd be delighted to walk with you to the school today. Our teacher, Miss Molly, is in Dallas buying new books for the children, giving them a day off from school. Our local carpenter, Hans Krinle, is building book shelves while the school house is closed. Would you like that?"

"Yes. I'd like to see where David learns his lessons." She smiled sweetly at Marie's husband. He was being so kind to her, causing a wave of jealousy through Marie. Was he the kind of man who would turn from his own wife for the looks of a pretty woman?

Constance hissed in her ear. "He looks smitten. I told you no one would want a woman like you."

Marie turned around to say something when she realized David was following in the rear. She held her breath, counted to five and clamped down on her jaw.

Between Owen charming the agent and Constance reminding her she wasn't worthy as a woman, she was close to an explosion of sorts. It was all Marie could do to keep her mouth tightly closed.

After approving of the place where David lived, They left the house and walked down the street towards the school house. Marie watched as *Winnie* tucked her hand through her husband's arm, furious at Owen for allowing it to go on this long. He was trying to be kind and yet the thought of something else stirring inside of him worried her. Constance didn't help.

Every move Owen made to charm Winnie, Constance nudged Marie's elbow. Halfway down the street, she lapse behind, walking with David and ignoring the others. It was a cold day in Hades before she allowed fear of losing her husband to overcome her. Marie was done with being scared of everything.

Even Constance. She finally had the nerve to speak up to her, with her father's approval it seemed. He had stayed behind, claiming to be tired. The truth was he probably wanted a few minutes away from his wife. Who could blame him for that?

As they walked down the street, Owen kept Winnie talking. They found out she was leaving shortly to go into Mill Ridge to catch the train. She didn't mean Zto impose, she told Owen, however she didn't want to miss her ride. They really didn't give her but a few hours to visit before she had to move on to the next family. "I'll be visiting several families on my way back. Kansas will be my first stop and then on to Ohio where two families have children there. It's a very satisfying job making sure the children are safe."

She kept on and on, while Owen listened intently. She told him if it were up to her, she'd prepare the family first, but the company policy was not hers. Marie was going to be sick if she kept on and on about imposing on his work as a doctor! He kept saying he didn't mind one bit.

Winnie also told them after they visited the school house, she had to be going since she left her carpet bag in the parlor of the boarding house. The proprietor had to clean the room for the next person.

Constance spoke up. "That means there will be a room available. Thank Goodness! I'll head there right now and secure a room for Lloyd and I."

Marie watched her hurry away, almost running to the boarding house. A wagon passed by them, stopping to pick up several people standing along the road. Good. It looked like the wagon that would take Winnie into Mill Ridge.

She was no longer worried they'd try to take David away. After all, Owen had charmed the woman so much, Marie was about to roll her eyes into her head. When they were alone she was going to give him a word or two.

Relief flooded through her knowing Constance went to secure the empty room. At least that woman would be out of their hair.

They toured the school quickly, then Winnie took her board and scribbled some notes. She handed the paper to Owen. "Please sign here that you acknowledged my visit. Congratulations, you've passed this inspection with flying colors."

Marie was ecstatic and didn't even care that she had been ignored by the agent through the whole visit.

David jumped up and down. "I can stay here?"

Marie had to give her credit. She leaned down to his eye level and gave him a pinch on the cheek. "Of course you can. I'm happy to know you are safe and will be well taken care of."

"Can I go play with my friends now?"

"That's up to your parents." She gazed at Owen. "I'm afraid I must go before the wagon gets here. Thank you for the excellent visit."

"Let me escort you to the boarding house. We can't have you walk alone."

Marie was done watching him act like a love-struck man. "I believe Cooper's Ridge is safe for Miss Winnie to walk by herself, Owen."

He slowed his steps. "Uh, oh. There is the wagon and it's leaving."

The three of them stood watching in complete shock as they watched the wagon get closer.

Marie's jaw dropped. "Is that Constance? What is she doing."

Her step-mother was laughing hysterically and waving an arm in the air. "I'm going to Kansas! Tell your father good luck and good riddance! She nudged the driver to move faster.

"Wait! I'm supposed to be on that wagon!" Winnie began to walk into the street. "I'll miss my train!"

The wagon master began to slow down when Constance waved a few bills in front of him. He turned back to Winnie. "I'm sorry ma'am. The wagon is full. I'll return in two days and pick you up."

"Two days!" Winnie looked terrified that she'd have to stay longer.

Marie felt horrified that Winnie would be stuck here so close to her husband.

"There's nothing you can do, Winnie. Let's get you back to the boarding house and let them know you'll need the room."

Marie agreed. There was no way they'd invite the agent into their home. As they passed the telegraph office, Winnie insisted they stop there first so she could let her home office know what happened. "I'm afraid I'll be delayed by a few days. I'll be lucky to keep my job," she mumbled, clearly upset at Constance taking her seat on the wagon.

While she went inside, Marie gazed down the street to check on David. He was across the street playing in the neighbor's front yard with his two friends. On the way back she'd remind him to be home before dark.

Owen was having a conversation with Pastor Murphy but his eyes were on Marie. He knew she wasn't too happy. Marie could see it in his eyes. It served him right, flirting with the agent like a man not married!

Owen's face fell when Cooper handed him a telegram. She watched as his jaw tightened and he let out a long sigh. "I guess it's time then," he said out loud.

"I hired a sheriff for the town. He's getting settled in now."

Owen shook his head. "What's a sheriff going to do, Cooper? We don't have a jail house or sheriff's office."

"We will. You're about to find out what our new sheriff can do. Get your family to the White Ranch within the next few hours."

Marie didn't hesitate. "What is happening? Is that horrible outlaw coming?" She took a hold of Owen's arm and shook it slightly. Everything was happening all at once. It was almost too much to bear.

Owen gave her a nod. "Yes. I want you to get David, take him home and warn your father. Take him along if he'll go. I'll be around in ten minutes with the buggy."

Marie was about to turn and find David when Winnie came out of the boarding house, angry as a rattlesnake about to attack. "That woman took my train ticket and my money. It's all gone! I want to speak with the law here!"

Pastor Murphy, wearing a gun belt low on his hips and black glove on his hands, pushed his black hat back and stared at the woman. It was more like a glare. The man looked more like an outlaw than a man of God. "Please, ma'am. Not right now!" he told her in a stern voice a preacher usually didn't talk in. "Sheriff Mac will be here any moment. We'll deal with it after we catch the outlaws that are about to show up. You best get inside for your own safety."

It didn't take much for Winnie to hike up her skirt and run for the boarding house.

Marie's head swirled in circles. It felt like the world was tilting on its axle and she was smack dab in the middle of chaos.

Constance stole from Winnie, who was pitching a fit on the street!

The outlaw was coming now instead of in a few weeks!

She had to get David to safety!

Marie had to tell her father his wife ran off and stole someone's belongings!

They had to leave here before it was too late.

She looked at Owen, who stared back in concern. "Go on. Please. Hurry!"

She was about to turn on her heels when Owen pulled her to him and kissed her in front of Winnie and Pastor Murphy like it was the last time he'd ever see or touch her.

She backed away, her finger tips against her swelled lips, scared of what was about to happen.

Chapter 16

Owen watched Marie run towards David, lean over and whisper in his ear, then tug him gently as they made their way across the street. The two ran up the steps and into the house. He turned to Cooper.

"How much time do I have?"

"I'm seriously not sure, Owen. Get moving. Stay with your family. We'll take care of business here."

"I'm making sure they're safe and coming back. It's time I face the music."

"If you insist, but the men with Vic are dangerous men. You may want to stay put. It also may be over by the time you return."

Owen shook his head. He wanted to end this once and for all.

Cooper sighed. "Go on. Get moving. Sheriff Mac will be here to help protect our town at any moment. Knowing him, he knows exactly where Vic and his gang are and will show his face at the last minute. We'll all protect what's ours, Owen. Go protect yours. The men of Wichita Falls and Mill Ridge are not staying idle. We plan to get rid of these varmints before they do any more damage."

Owen had turned to go when he swung around. "How did they get so far this quickly? I thought those men you talked about were going to make sure they didn't get through so fast without notice?"

"You have a lot to learn, Owen. Nothing ever goes according to plan. That's why God gave us guns and ammunition."

Owen wasn't sure that was an appropriate answer, but he practically ran down to the livery and hitched up his horse and buggy. When he got to his house, Marie, her father and David were all waiting on the porch. It looked as if she haphazardly shoved clothes in her old carpet bag.

They all climbed on the wagon, with Marie in the front and David and Lloyd in the back. "I'm sorry about your wife leaving, Lloyd," Owen told him, sincerely meaning those words. "But we have bigger fish to fry. The White Ranch will be a safe haven for all of you. If the outlaws know I have family, every one of you may be in danger."

Lloyd snorted. "Glad to be rid of that old nag. Probably the best thing I've done is come out here to Cooper's Ridge. I wonder if there will ever be a bank here?"

"It may be the perfect place to start one, sir. It's a little rough around the edges but people have to put their money somewhere instead of going all the way to Wichita Falls."

Lloyd nodded. "It might be, son."

It only took an hour to get to the White Ranch but it seemed so much longer. Owen kept looking over his shoulder for any sign of danger. He knew there was a shotgun under the bench and it would be easy to grab it and fire. It was the last thing he wanted to do, harm another human being.

He was a doctor. He healed people. But Vic Townsly was a man who didn't care how he felt. He'd shoot first and ask questions afterwards.

Owen's life was right here in this wagon. He loved Marie with all his heart and soul. He'd do whatever it takes to keep them out of harm's way, including killing another man.

He pulled the buggy to the front door. Nora was already outside, a shotgun in her arms. Rusty, her husband, had gathered up a few of the ranch hands, instructing a few men to guard the road leading to the ranch. He also had some men scattered around the property.

Owen felt good about leaving them in their hands. When Marie looked back after helping her father down from the buggy, her eyes blinked rapidly. She knew he wasn't going to stay. He saw it in her face.

"I'm sorry, Marie. I have to go back and take care of business."

She held out her hand and took one of his. "You come back to me, Owen. Or, I'll come looking for you."

"Stay put, Marie. I'll come back to you, I promise."

His eyes darted to Nora, who was standing on the porch. "Make sure she stays right here, no matter what."

Nora nodded. "Go on, now. You've got a job to do."

As he rode away, Owen wasn't sure if he'd be able to keep his promise to come back to his wife. He'd sure give it a good try. As long as the ones he loved were safe, it didn't much matter if he lived or died. He wanted to live. The Lord knew he wanted to.

Guess it's a good time to ask your favor, Lord. I've been a lonely man most of my life. I've tried to atone for taking Charlie Townsly's life even though he would've killed me. I pray now that you intervene so I don't have to kill another man. It leaves me with a bad taste in my mouth. I want to heal people. It's my gift. You have the last word. Amen.

Owen probably pushed the horse a little too hard but he wanted to get back to Cooper's Ridge. As he was coming around one turn, four men on horses waved him down. At first he thought it was Townsly. His arm reached under the bench for his shotgun until he recognized Sheriff Nightengale from Mill Ridge.

"Hold up, Owen. We're coming with you." Two of the other men got off their horses and jumped in the back of the wagon with the sheriff. One man stayed with the horses.

THE RUNAWAY

"Don't bring the horses in too early," the sheriff called out. "Give us about fifteen minutes. This won't take long."

Owen had no idea what was going on. All he knew was three men were covered up with a tarp in the back of his wagon. "Mind telling me what we're doing?"

"Nope. Just follow along, Owen. I'll apologize now for putting you in this position."

"What position. Wait a minute! What is happening?"

The sheriff had his head poking out of the tarp. "Cooper Murphy just sent Vic Townsly and his men this way, knowing you'd be on your way back to town. He didn't want bloodshed around innocent folk."

"I'm riding right into an ambush? What if I'd have stayed at the ranch?"

"We all knew better, Owen. You are a man of integrity. We knew you'd follow your conscience and face Townsly. Well, I'd say you are about to. Look ahead." He slid back down under the tarp. "Get ready men."

Owen was sweating bullets. Four men were coming his way, riding beside each other blocking the road. There was no way he'd be able to bypass them. He began to slow down his buggy.

A muffled sound came from under the tarp. "When we say now, you get down, Owen. Let the experts do their job."

Owen watched the men come to a stop. They all held a rifle in their arm. The buggy came to a dead stop. He didn't say a word. Everything felt like it was in slow motion, like the outlaws knew that Owen knew what they were there for.

"They holding rifles or pistols, Owen?"

Owen mumbled to hide the fact he was talking to someone. "Rifles."

"Okay, men. On the count of five. Ready. One. Two. Three."

"At the count of three instead of five, the tarp flew off, Owen flattened himself on the bench and the sheriff and his men began shooting. They never spoke a word. Owen reached under his bench and pulled out the rifle, waiting until the gunfire stopped before he popped his head up and aimed the rifle.

It was all over. Four men were lying on the ground. Dead. Sheriff Nightengale patted Owen on the shoulder. "It's all over, Doc. Sorry we didn't have time to tell you about our plan. Sometimes it's better if you don't know."

In this case, it probably was. The men in the back jumped out of his buggy. One of them turned to Owen and held out his hand. "That's how we keep the riff-raff out of Cooper's Ridge. I'm your new sheriff, Bartholomew McAlister. My friends call me Mac."

*****

"Has anyone seen David?" Marie was getting worried. David and Goliath were both missing. She'd checked the barn several times in the last hour but they were nowhere to be found. She thought the boy was with one of the cowboys until she saw that same cowboy ride out of the lane.

That's when she got nervous and began to look for him everywhere. Rusty was on the porch with Nora, drinking lemonade. They both sat there with a shotgun across their lap. "We sent a few of our men to Cooper's Ridge to check on things." Rusty and Nora looked concerned when she told them she hadn't been able to find David.

"He was here and it seems like he just disappeared. I thought he was in the barn with one of the ranch hands, but I saw the ranch hand ride away, alone."

Rusty got up and headed towards the barn. "I'll check for you, ma'am. Sometimes kids hide in the barn."

Marie followed him. Nora stood guard on the porch. After searching for ten minutes, they came up empty-handed. That's when Rusty noticed one of the ponies was missing. "Beans is missing," he shouted to Nora. "I'm gonna saddle up and go look for her. I have a notion that's where the boy is."

"Do you think he is riding Beans? He doesn't know how to ride."

"Beans' saddle is missing, too," he pointed out. "I'm pretty certain he got a hankering to ride. He was told to never go alone, so I'm not sure why he went against our orders."

Marie rung her hands while Rusty saddled up one of the geldings. "Kids will be kids. We'll find him. Don't worry. I doubt he got too far."

"It's been a rough time for him. He finally found a good home with us and then everything turned to chaos. He's probably scared. David has a history of running away."

The fear that he was out on the ranch lost somewhere terrified her. She tried hard to stay calm and breathe. She wanted Owen so badly it felt like a weight was crushing her heart.

Rusty rode off while Marie went back to Nora. "I can't just sit here and wait. This is the worst."

Nora pointed with her rifle. "I don't think you have to. Look, here comes your husband."

The buggy was coming in fast down the lane, the wheels kicking up a cloud of dust behind it.

Marie took off down the steps, running through the yard. Owen called out, bringing the buggy to a stop. She fell into his arms, so happy to see him. "Oh, thank you, Lord for bringing him back to me!"

"I told you I'd be back." Owen held her so tight she could hardly breathe.

"You did keep your promise. I have to admit I was concerned. There's trouble here, Owen. It's David. He's missing."

Owen stiffened. "What do you mean, he's missing?" His tone was hard and he stood rigid, thinking the worst, she was sure.

"I don't know. He was supposed to be in the barn with one of the men here. When I went to find him, he was gone. One of the little ponies is gone too."

Nora had ordered one of the hands to saddle up a horse when she saw Owen coming down the lane, sure he wanted to help in the search for David. He nodded his thanks and helped Marie up behind him. She clung onto his waist, not wanting to ever let him go.

"Lou will go with you. He can catch up to Rusty. Don't worry, we'll find him."

They followed behind Lou, looking everywhere. For over an hour they searched then came upon Rusty, who was starting to be concerned. "It will get dark in about two hours. We'll have to cover more ground.

Before they split up, a soft neigh came from a row of trees near one of the streams nearby. "Did you hear that?"

Owen nodded. He cautiously walked the horse to where the sound was coming from. He pointed.

Marie almost shrieked when she saw David lying in the grass beside the pony. She slid from the horse without assistance and ran towards the boy. "David? Are you all right?"

The boy stirred. When he turned his head, there was blood in his hair and running down his temple. That's when she did shriek. Owen went by her, checking the wound first, then lifting the boy in his arms. "Let's get him back to the ranch."

They rode fast and hard until they got back to the house. Nora immediately saw the boy was hurt and motioned them inside. She instructed Owen to place him in the room off the kitchen area and went to heat up water.

Marie was holding David's hand, reassuring him everything will be all right. But, would it be ever again? The boy was fading in and out of consciousness one too many times for her. What if he had brain damage from the fall? It would be her fault for not making him stay by her side. "This is my fault," she whispered. "I'm so sorry, David."

Owen's gentle hand cupped her cheek. "Boys defy rules until they get caught. I don't know what triggered him to take off like that when he knew better than to ride a horse on his own, but we're going to find out. Take a look."

David's eyes were open. They were a bit glazed, but he was staring at Marie. When he saw Owen, a huge smile replaced the stoned look on his face. "You came back!"

He reached up and wrapped his arms around Owen's neck. "Of course I came back, David. I told you I would."

"I was so afraid, Father."

Marie witnessed a miracle. Owen had a tear in his eye as she watched the two embrace. He gazed into Marie's eyes. Did you hear that? he mouthed.

She nodded, her tears flowing freely. She patted her son on the back. "We'll never leave you, David. You have to know by now you are a huge part of our family."

"I know. But that lady kept telling me that I was no good and no one wants an orphan."

"What lady?" She thought at first he meant Nora. She was ready to defend her son no matter who owned this ranch.

"Grandpa's mean wife."

Owen hugged David a little tighter. Marie laughed. "You don't have to worry about that woman any longer. She left town earlier and won't be back. We won't let her come back, David."

"Good. 'Cause I was getting worried. When you didn't come back I thought maybe that lady said something mean to you, too and you didn't want to come back to me. I just wanted to run away."

Marie and Owen looked at each other. "David. We promise never to leave you. Do you believe me?"

"I think so."

Owen chimed in. "No one would ever or could ever say anything that will change my mind."

Marie spoke up with the news she'd been keeping to herself. "Besides, young man, your little brother or sister will want to get to know you."

Owen stopped. His mouth dropped and his jaw hung open. "Are you sure?"

When she nodded, he shook his head. "Have you seen a doctor?"

She laughed out loud. "I think the doctor caused this." She placed a hand across her mid-section.

Owen grinned. He placed his hand over top of hers. "We're going to have a baby."

David's little hand went on top of his fathers. "We're all having a baby?"

Marie hugged him. "Yes, we are. We'll all be one happy family. Are you ready to go home, David?"

He looked up at his father. When Owen nodded, David looked at her and nodded, too. Just like his father.

Marie was in tears. Her runaway son finally realized where he belonged. He'd never have to run away again.

*****

Thank you for reading **The Runaway**, the first book in the Outlaws & Orphans of Cooper's Ridge series. It's always so much fun creating a new series. Are you ready for Book 2?

A Man Wanting To Change His Ways - A Woman Forced to Start Over - An Innocent Child Full of Shenanigans!

There's a new sheriff in town and he has his eye on everything. Including the children's agent stranded at the boarding house. He vows to keep Cooper's Ridge free from riff-raff. As a former bounty hunter and soldier, Sheriff Mac is ready to settle down, start a family and change his wandering ways.

When a harrowed wife from a neighboring farm gives the orphan she ordered back to the children's agent claiming the child is a spawn of the devil, Winnie has a decision to make. Without a home to go back to or a job, will Winnie accept Sheriff Mac's offer of marriage of convenience or leave at the first chance she gets?

AVAILABLE NOW!

Book 2 - The Mischief Maker[1]

(https://www.amazon.com/dp/B09WJDVKXM)

---

[1]. https://www.amazon.com/dp/B09WJDVKXM

Don't miss out!

Visit the website below and you can sign up to receive emails whenever Cyndi Raye publishes a new book. There's no charge and no obligation.

https://books2read.com/r/B-A-PXQ-KPPEC

BOOKS2READ

Connecting independent readers to independent writers.

Printed in the USA
CPSIA information can be obtained
at www.ICGtesting.com
LVHW040016200624
783498LV00010B/504